THE UNEXPECTED!

. . . Out in the yard was a big, old open truck painted dirty yellow and filthy white that belonged to the Pine Ridge Township sanitation department. Mom was standing at the living-room window, gazing out at the scene with complete rapture.

"Dad's getting rid of his junk after all, huh?" I said, going over to watch alongside her.

"Rid?" she said absently, "rid? Oh no, baby, no, that stuff's all going with us."

"*With* us?"

"Uh huh."

"In *that?*"

"Uh huh."

"In a garbage truck?"

"Uh huh."

"We're going to drive across the United States, to New York, in a garbage truck?"

"Uh huh. Got it cheap as dirt from the township. Isn't it just splendid! Big and sturdy and tough, with a roomy cab for the three of us to sit in. And enough space to carry everything. Can you honestly think of anything better?"

And to tell you the truth, considering my family and all, I honestly couldn't. . . .

ME AND
FAT GLENDA

ME AND
FAT GLENDA

Lila Perl

AN ARCHWAY PAPERBACK
Published by POCKET BOOKS • NEW YORK

An Archway Paperback published by
POCKET BOOKS, a division of Simon & Schuster, Inc
1230 Avenue of the Americas, New York, N.Y. 10020

Published by arrangement with The Seabury Press
Library of Congress Catalog Card Number: 71-179439

ISBN: 0-671-49868-1

First Pocket Books printing August, 1973

10 9 8 7 6

IN MY family I'm always the last person to find out anything. For instance, the way I found out we were moving from California to New York was by overhearing Mrs. Hinkle and Mrs. Bruntley talking in the supermarket. In other words, I was eavesdropping. Only those two always talked so loud you didn't have to feel the least bit sneaky about listening.

"Just this morning it was, she told me," Mrs. Hinkle was saying. "Came and stood in the doorway as I was sweeping the front walk. Yessiree, there she stood in one of those black spider outfits of hers with her hair hanging down like drapery tassels all over her face.

" 'We'll be vacating at the end of the month, Mrs. Hinkle,' says she. 'Drew has a teaching job at a college in New York State.' "

That was my mother Mrs. Hinkle was talking about. Mom does wear a black leotard most of the time with a short smock or a sleeveless tunic over it made out of some kind of hand-blocked material in bright, contrasty colors. And she does wear her hair long and fringelike, with chopped-off clumps here and there around her face.

But so what?

Drew, the man my mother mentioned, he's my father. And, oh, I should explain that Mrs. Hinkle was our landlady. We had been renting out the right-hand side of her double-size frame house on a shady side street not far from the college for about a year and a half now.

I sort of snuggled up against the catfood in Aisle 3 and kept right on listening. Hinkle and Bruntley were standing in Aisle 4.

"Well, won't you be happy to see them go?" Mrs. Bruntley asked in a loud whisper. "All those parties with the dancing and the blinking lights. They must've ruined your floorboards."

I got a little mad at that one because the truth was Mrs. Hinkle's floorboards weren't much to begin with. The whole house was so infested with termites that a piece of it seemed to break off nearly every other day. Besides, the house had mice—and Mrs. Hinkle knew it. There were nests of field mice under the porch foundation and under the broken back steps and even behind the wooden boards under the kitchen sink. Not many people in California would be caught living in a dilapidated old house like that anymore.

Mrs. Hinkle, who was probably feeling bad about the house and wondering whom she would ever find to rent it to next, said, "Well, all of these

2

college people, professors and the like ~~pixilated these days."

But Mrs. Bruntley kept right on ~~Hinkle what was wrong with us Mayberrys. (Me— by the way—I'm Sara Mayberry.)

"Now you know very well, La Verne, that those Mayberrys are the *most* pixilated you ever had in that house of yours. Him with that beard and those sandals and all that junk piled up and nailed together in the backyard that's supposed to be art or sculpture or heaven-only-knows-what. And that high-school boy of theirs is just as bad. The spitting image of the father except no beard—yet. Of course I do feel just a wee bit sorry for that girl of theirs. She seems normal. Can't think why."

"Yeah," Mrs. H. agreed. "Too bad about that. Nice little thing. Not *too* pixilated. Well, I have to be getting on."

I had to be getting on, too, so I waved good-bye to Hinkle and Bruntley even though they couldn't see me. I did peek around Aisle 4 though just in time to catch a last glimpse of them in their hairnets and their brown walking oxfords and flower-print dresses fading away in the direction of CANNED SOUPS and SOAPS AND DETERGENTS.

I was shaken up, of course, by the news. But for the moment I had to concentrate on my shopping, too. It was the day for D-burgers and I still didn't know what D was going to stand for.

3

I guess I should explain about the alphabet-burgers. It was an idea Toby and I had cooked up. (Toby is the "spitting image" high-school boy without the "beard—yet," and he also happens to be my brother.) Since Inez and Drew (Mom and Pop) had come off their Mexican-food kick—which was mostly *guacamole,* a sloshy avocado mash, and re-fried beans—they were on a raw-food kick and *that* was really rough. Raw mushrooms, raw cauliflower, raw zucchini, and—worst of all—raw fish.

"After it's taken a bath in lime juice, of course," Inez had said the first time she tried to get me to taste it. According to my mother the lime juice really "cooked" the fish. It was an old South Seas recipe. But the fish still tasted raw and slimy to me.

So what with all that, and some of the other sick-ening food kicks they'd been on, I'd gotten hit with doing most of the cooking for Toby and me for a couple of years now. Only what did I know about cooking? Hamburgers. Those were my big specialty. And could they ever get monotonous!

So that was why we invented the alphabet-burger. We had only just started on it the week before. A was apple-burgers. Fried apple slices, sprinkled with sugar and cinnamon, slapped on top of the hamburgers and eaten on toasted buns. Not bad.

Toby liked the apple-burgers so much he thought B should be banana-burgers. But I didn't go for that at all, so we had bean-burgers. Baked beans where the fried apples had been the time before.

4

C was easy—cheeseburgers. It was so easy I felt guilty. I figured we would go through the alphabet twice just to make it harder. I wasn't even thinking of letters such as X, Y, and Z at the time.

D was really hard, even the first time around. D, D, D . . . I could see I'd be wandering up and down the aisles of that supermarket for a long, long time.

By the time I got home it was nearly suppertime because I hadn't even begun my supermarket shopping until after school. Mom was already packing her leotards and Pop was in the backyard dismantling the largest and most gruesome of his junk sculptures.

"Some of this metalwork is priceless," he remarked to Mom when he stomped into the kitchen once between derivetings. "You know, I," (that was short for Inez) "I'll never be able to find anything even remotely resembling this stuff in New York. Historically speaking, the Eastern seaboard predates the West Coast by over 200 years. Everything worthwhile in the East must have been grabbed up ages ago. Why these iron spikes from the Union Pacific Railroad alone are worth a fortune."

Needless to say, Pop planned to take all his junk to New York with him for "redesign and reconstruction" and Mom had sweetly assented to this. She wasn't really in a position to object. She had a few things to lug East herself—her loom (very handy for weaving rugs and carpets and the like), her dyeing vats and wax-melting pots for hand-blocking and batik-making (which Mrs. Hinkle had once rather witchily referred to as her "caul-drons"), an old harpsichord, an old harp, an old zither, and a few other broken-down musical instruments that she had been collecting over the years and was forever promising to put into "proper playing order."

"Doesn't matter, though," Inez remarked breez-ily when I pointed out how loaded we would be on the trip East. "Think, just think Sara love, of all the space we'll be saving by not taking any cooking pots with us at all." (She was wrong there. I wasn't going anywhere without my hamburger grill.) "Oh, I tell you baby, eating food in its natural state beats all, from every possible point of view. Just give *that* a think."

And sure enough, a few minutes later Inez and Drew sank down cross-legged on the living-room floor and ate their dinner—raw chopped meat sprinkled with raw chopped onions, and, on top of that, two gloppy raw egg yolks!

Meantime, Toby got in from late session at the high school. I started to tell him the news, but he already knew. He'd heard about it late that morn-ing before leaving for school—which explained why no one had told me. I left for school at eight o'clock, and Drew had only gotten the letter and phoned Mom at around ten.

I fried the D-burgers, and Toby and I sat down to eat at the kitchen table. Toby kept shaking his head back and forth as he ate. Oh, he liked the D-burgers all right. It was the moving to New York that had him upset.

"Can't do," Toby said. "Felipe and I discussed it and we're still going on this digging expedition to Mexico this summer."

"You mean you're not coming East with us?"

"That's right," Toby said. And I knew from looking into his eyes, which are the darkest possible brown without being actually black, and at the set of his jaw, which is "pronounced" even when he's asleep, that he really meant it.

Even if Toby is my brother, I have to admit that he isn't the least bit handsome. He isn't even good-looking. But he's what I would call really great to look at. He has sort of craggy features with a slightly crooked nose and a slightly crooked mouth, a face that's both rough and tender all at the same time. His hair is wavy and brown, and he wears it kind of low on his forehead and full all around but not really long.

I can tell that girls are crazy about him because all the time I keep getting more and more girl-friends, even some of the stuck-up ones from Pine Ridge Drive who suddenly start developing an interest in looms and zithers and junk sculpture just as an excuse to hang around our place and keep an eye out for Toby.

"Oh well," I said resignedly, "I guess you'll get your way. Pop's pretty sympathetic to archaeology and Mexico and all that stuff."

Toby nodded and I realized he was caring just a little bit about my having to go it alone with Inez and Drew to New York.

"Sorry kid," he said, grabbing another D-burger. "I'll sure miss your cooking, but I like it fine here in California. In the fall I'll probably move in with Felipe's family and finish out my last year of high school out here instead of making still another switch."

So that meant Toby would be trading my cooking for Mrs. Gonzaga's. Felipe's mother was a good cook all right—if you liked Mexican food. Which Toby did. Which I didn't.

Still I couldn't blame Toby. He'd already had enough gypsying around to last anyone else a lifetime. Because he was five years older than I was, Inez and Drew had really lugged him all over— Peru, on a special two-year expedition to try to uncover an ancient Inca secret that it turned out even the ancient Incas didn't have the answer to; Thailand, so Drew could write a doctoral thesis on the hill tribes who smeared lipstick all over their cheeks instead of on their lips and whose children all smoked pipes; Albania, where Drew wanted to study the inheritance customs of the Ghegs and the Tosks.

It sure had made a mess of Toby's education, and if he wasn't a natural-born genius he'd have been in fourth grade at age 16-going-on-17 instead of in his junior year in high school.

During most of the Mayberry travels I either wasn't born yet or got left behind with Pop's Aunt Minna in Crestview, Ohio. Now that was a nice normal place, Crestview. In some ways Aunt Minna was a more pleasant version of Mrs. Hinkle and with a much nicer house. All sunshiny smiles, starched white curtains, milk and fresh doughnuts every afternoon after school, and roast chicken with mashed potatoes and gravy on Sunday—that was Aunt Minna.

Inez didn't exactly approve of Aunt Minna. "A narrow-minded old fuddy-duddy," Inez called her, "who'll hand the child creature comforts while lulling her mind to sleep and instilling all sorts of prejudices."

Aunt Minna *was* pretty straight I guess. Just a nice older lady who watched television a lot and went to church suppers and had never traveled farther than Columbus (Ohio—not Christopher). But sometimes I got homesick for her and for Crestview after Inez and Drew and Toby came back from that last trip (to a Greek island called Astypalaia where Pop was making a survey of life styles among the sponge fishermen) and we set up house in California.

"So when will I ever see you again?" I said to Toby, leaning forward with both elbows on the table and my woebegone face between my palms. "I mean after we leave here, which is like two weeks from now."

Toby grinned that crooked little grin of his that makes you love him and hate him at the exact same moment. "Oh, don't worry," he said, getting up from the table and hitching up his Levi's. "I'll see ya around." He gave me a sort of mock punch on the chin—for love, I guess.

Just at that moment Mom exclaimed from the living room, "They're here!"

I got up and ran to the kitchen windows, which like all the windows in our house had no curtains or shades or blinds on them because Inez said windows were to SEE through. But all I saw out in the yard was a big, old open truck painted dirty yellow and filthy white that belonged to the Pine Ridge Township sanitation department.

"Hey, what do you know," I remarked to Toby who was already out of the room, "Pop's giving up his junk after all."

But the two figures that jumped down from the cab of the truck weren't garbage men at all. They were friends of Drew—beards, sandals, Levi's, the usual bit. In no time at all, Pop was out there with them and they were all three heaving the disassembled junk into the back of the truck.

Inez was standing at the living-room window, gazing out at the scene with complete rapture and murmuring over and over again, "Marvelous, marvelous, marvelous."

"He's getting rid of it after all, huh?" I said, going over to watch alongside her.

"Rid?" she said absently, "rid? Oh no, baby, no, that stuff's all going with us." And she seemed so happy she crouched down and put her arm around my shoulders and hugged me.

"With us?"

"Uh huh."

"In *that?"*

"Uh huh."

"In a garbage truck?"

"Uh huh."

"We're going to drive across the United States, to New York, in a garbage truck?"

"Uh huh. Got it cheap as dirt from the township. They're putting in a whole new fleet. With enclosed bodies and interior grinding apparatus—oh, you know the kind. But isn't this one just splendid! Big and sturdy and tough, with a roomy cab for the three of us to sit in. And enough space to carry everything. Can you honestly think of anything better?"

And to tell you the truth, considering my family and all, I honestly couldn't.

But even so, as I watched through the window, angry tears spurted from my eyes. And through the blur, bigger than life, I could just see us all—Drew and Inez and me, Sara—riding all the way from California to New York in a grimy yellow and white garbage truck with the words DEPARTMENT OF SANITATION, PINE RIDGE TOWNSHIP, COLONNA COUNTY, CALIFORNIA, printed in big black letters on both sides of it.

P.S. I guess I never did say what the D in D-burger stood for.

The answer is dog. Not for dogfood (although I thought of that; some of it is real tasty). D is for dog like in hot dog. Sliced crosswise into circles, fried, and sprinkled on top of the hamburgers. And let me tell you, dog-burgers are GOOD.

S. M.

2

WELL, I won't even tell you about the ride across the U. S. in the PINE RIDGE TOWNSHIP garbage truck except to say that it took six weeks and people kept giving us odder and odder looks the farther we got from California.

The reason it took six weeks wasn't only because a garbage truck is about as fast-moving as a sea turtle in the Arabian desert, or because we had to use a lot of back roads because of different state turnpike regulations. It also took six weeks because we kept hopping from the house of one friend or relative of Drew or Inez to another.

And each place we stayed we spent a couple of days getting cleaned up, rinsing out our jeans and leotards and waiting for them to dry, and most of all waiting for the vibrations in our bone marrow to stop. Then back in the truck we'd climb and the whole thing would start all over again.

You have to understand that Drew had a lot of friends who seemed to be sprinkled across the United States like stepping stones across a river. And whenever there was a little too much space between the stones for a convenient jump, there was always a relative of Inez to fill in the gap.

This was easy because Mom is one of the most mixed-blooded persons you're ever likely to meet. She's part Irish, part German, part French-Canadian, and part American Indian—just for a start. The first night out from home we stayed with one of her third cousins on an Indian reservation in Arizona. We also made stops with Mom's relations in Nebraska and Wisconsin and we even looped up into Canada to see some of the French great-aunts and uncles. But the one place we didn't go was Crestview, Ohio.

"It's completely out of the way," Inez declared when I suggested it and Drew said why didn't we at least give it a "maybe."

"No," Inez said with finality. "We'll *never* get to New York at this rate."

Well, if I ever showed you a diagram of our route from California to New York, you'd think a giant serpent had been wriggling its way across the U. S. Out of our way? What way? A bunch of crazy curlicues that inched along in the general direction known as east.

So I never did get to see Aunt Minna again. Pop tried to be consoling, especially when I cried a lot in Pittsburgh after I got hold of the road map and found out we were only about an inch and a quarter away from Crestview, Ohio.

Even with all the people we kept stopping off to

see, and lots of them with kids my age, the trip was awfully lonely. Then, too, all of my friends from California were left behind, probably forever, and I didn't know if I would find any new ones when we got to New York.

Most of all I missed Toby. Every time I ate a hamburger I thought of him, and you can imagine how often that was, since I practically lived on hamburgers the whole time. Toby and I had stopped our alphabet-burgers at the letter K (kraut-burgers), and I knew I just wouldn't have the heart to go on with the alphabet-burgers without him.

So, all in all, I was just as glad the day we rolled into Mill River, Long Island, New York, where the college was. All the buildings—if you can imagine this—were built in California Spanish-mission style and painted banana-yellow!

Inez took one look at them and laughed so hard she thought her leotards would split. "That architecture makes about as much sense as calling this place Mill River. It hasn't got a mill anywhere in sight, and there isn't a river within leagues of the place. Bays and oceans and sounds all around, but no river."

Well, *we* looked pretty silly, too. The truck was by now the color of U. S. road dust that had been patty-caked by rain into an all-over coating of mud (which was a blessing because it covered the lettering on the sides). The college guard wouldn't let us on the campus and made us drive around to the service entrance when Drew wanted to report to the administration office and find out about our housing.

Pop was gone a pretty long time, and when he came back he didn't say a word, just climbed into the truck and started shifting gears.

"Where is it?" I asked, looking around at the wide gravel drives and big empty lawns that surrounded the three-story banana buildings. "Is it near?" There were still three weeks to go before the college opened for fall classs and the place was almost deserted.

"I just hope it's spacious and roomy," Inez remarked. "I don't care if it doesn't have a stick of furniture in it. As long as it's not one of those little boxes divided into compartments like an egg crate. Most of the houses I've seen here in the East looked pretty discouraging."

Pop muttered something, and Mom said, "What?"

"I said," Drew repeated rather louder than was necessary, "you won't like it."

Inez got that wide-eyed expression that usually meant trouble.

We were still within sight of the campus, driving past a long, low two-story building that looked like an army barracks, when Drew began slowing down. Pretty soon he stopped altogether. From the way he was squinting through the window of the truck

16

cab, you could tell he was trying to make out an address.

"Se-ven-tee *four*. That's it."

"No!" Inez exploded after a short pause. "I won't. I won't live in a box. I'll live in a truck. I'll live in a field. I'll even live in a tent. But I won't live in a box!"

"It's not a box," Drew said quietly. "It's a 'garden apartment.' We've got the one on the upper-floor. Five rooms. A lot of the college faculty who are on short-term contracts live here."

"Not me."

"It's only for a year."

"Never."

"It gets cold in the winter in New York, I. This place has steam heat."

"No."

"It has a completely remodeled modern kitchen, with a wall oven."

"What do I care? We don't need a kitchen. We eat raw food. Remember?"

"*I* don't," I reminded Inez.

"Well, you should," she snapped. "It's healthier."

"Let's just look at it anyway," Pop suggested.

"Yes, let's," I urged. It was a steamy-hot day and I was dying for a shower. Any place with a wall oven was sure to have a bathroom—and those *were* necessary. But Inez never seemed to think about things like that.

Besides, a few people had passed by and had looked up at the truck with curiosity. One lady was peering down at us from an upstairs window in the apartment next to ours, and another woman who was weeding a flower bed on the Kleenex-sized lawn in front of her apartment kept looking up at us through a clump of dangling weeds.

"All right," Inez said at last. "I'll look but I won't like—and I won't stay. They definitely wrote you they would provide housing. This is not a house. It's not even a box."

"That's true," Drew said. "It's not a house. It's housing. There's a difference. You should have looked that up, I, while we were still back in California, before you went jumping to conclusions."

"I won't unpack," Inez said after she'd made a quick tour of the five rooms furnished with colonial-style furniture that probably would have looked better somewhere else. (In a colonial-style house, I guess.) The rooms weren't really so little, though, and I myself thought the place could have been fixed up to be rather cosy for a normal family. But we Mayberrys weren't a normal family, so that put an end to that.

Drew kept staring out the rear windows of the apartment.

"That does it," he said after awhile. *"We* won't unpack."

"Oh, I'm glad to hear you say that," Inez exclaimed.

Drew kept right on staring out the window and shaking his head in disbelief and disappointment. "I thought there'd be a big expanse of ground back there, a place where a person could do a little construction. There's nothing. Just a roadway directly behind the buildings and then a string of garages."

"We'll camp," Inez said excitedly. "We won't unpack. We'll just camp, right here in the —ugh— apartment. And we'll go scouting every day. There must be real towns around here somewhere, with real houses in them. I thought I spotted a few rustic-looking places after we left the Expressway this morning. There are three weeks to go before classes begin and before school starts for Sara. I'm sure we'll find some place to live."

And there was Mom consoling Pop as though he'd been the one to practically throw a temper tantrum at the start. Of course all this talk about to-unpack-or-not-to-unpack was silly. The apartment was already pretty full of furniture and there was no attic or basement or backyard shed, so how *could* we unload looms and zithers and iron spikes from the Union Pacific Railroad? We just brought in our clothes and got ready to spend a couple of nights there, just as though we were still traveling across the U. S. on our way to somewhere.

Next day Pop got some maps of the nearby towns around the college and talked to a few people, and the administration office said they'd give him an allotment equal to the rent of the apartment toward the monthly rental of any house he found, Which meant the house had to be for rent at a pretty cheap price.

After about three days of cruising around in the nearby towns, Drew had to go get more maps. Most of the houses close to the college were already rented or owned by the college professors who had long-term contracts. Those that were left were either too expensive or else they were egg crates.

Inez said it wouldn't matter even if we moved to a town that was ten or fifteen miles away from the campus, since Drew would have the truck for daily transportation. She herself always used a bicycle for shopping and other errands.

One thing we found out from driving slowly through a lot of small town streets is that people are always glad to see the garbage man. Even though Drew had washed down the truck and it was now back to being filthy white and dirty yellow with big black letters that said it belonged to PINE RIDGE TOWNSHIP in California, you'd be surprised how many people came running out of their houses with bags of garbage as soon as they heard us coming.

One little old lady raced out with a whole bedsheet full of watermelon peels and cantaloupe rinds.

"My, I'm glad you came by this afternoon," she said brightly. "Not one of your regular pickups, is it? Well, you couldn't have picked a better time. I'm just putting up my watermelon pickle and I'm so glad to be getting rid of the garbage today before the weekend comes on. Bedsheet's old, too, so I thought that might as well go. You won't be coming by again a little later, will you? I'll have shrimp shells."

She looked almost ready to cry, standing there on the sidewalk with her torn, bulging bedsheet, after Pop told her we weren't taking any garbage, only looking for a nice roomy house to rent.

On the other hand, Drew picked up some fantastic junk, even though he had expected the pickings to be slim in the East. One man who had some big black stovepipes sitting out on the sidewalk flagged us down and then asked if we'd like to take a peek in his garage. Inez got a couple of enormous old tubs and dye pots out of that one and also a lyre with three strings missing.

But although junk kept piling up in the truck, we didn't seem to be getting any closer to finding a place where we would be able to unload it all. By now we were looking around in a town called Havenhurst, about fourteen miles from the college. Like most of the towns we had looked through, it had a mixture of old houses and new houses, a dilapidated old shopping street called Broadway, and a whopping big, neon-lit shopping center called the Havenhurst Shoppers Mall.

We were grinding past a spread-out new ranch

house with manicured grass and a red-and-white painted jockey on the lawn when a girl came running down the driveway, all the time yelling over her shoulder, "Hey Ma, the garbage man!"

Only Drew and I were in the truck that day. Inez had gone bicycling to a patch of woods on the north edge of the campus to hunt for mushrooms.

"Step on it," I said to Pop. "It's garbage this time for sure. Judging from the size of that kid, they eat a lot in that house."

Because this girl was fat. And when I say fat, I don't mean *fat*. I mean FAT.

"Hey wait, mister," the fat girl yelled, puffing her way toward us like a steam engine. "Please wait." And to my surprise, Drew began slowing to a stop. Not because of her, but because just ahead of us at the corner of the street, half hidden by trees, sat an old silvery gray wooden house in the middle of a weed-grown yard and surrounded by a fence with a lot of the pickets missing. And nailed to the fence was a big, tired-looking sign that said THIS PROPERTY FOR SALE OR RENT: Inquire Calvin Creasey, 108 Broadway, Havenhurst.

By now the fat girl was peering up into the cab of the truck, her cheeks and chin still shaking like jelly from that exhausting run down the driveway and along the street to the truck, maybe a whole twelve yards.

"Gee thanks for waiting, mister," she gasped up at Drew. "My mother'll be out in a minute. See, we

22

missed the pickup yesterday and our Dispose-all's on the blink."

"Forget it," I said, leaning over Pop's shoulder to save him the trouble for once. "We don't take garbage."

"You don't?" She looked pretty mad. Her hair, which was blonde and crinkly, seemed to stand up on end and her eyes, which were the same light hazel color as the freckles all over her cheeks, seemed to turn about three shades darker. She wasn't bad-looking and I figured she must have been just about my age—eleven, or maybe twelve. But as I said before, was she ever FAT.

"Then what are you riding around in a garbage truck for?" she wanted to know.

"That's our business," Drew snapped. He was getting tired of explanations, and what with school opening for me in just one week and classes starting at the college very soon after, the whole thing was getting to be a drag.

"It's a long story," I said apologetically.

"Listen," Drew said wearily to the fat girl. "What can you tell us about that house, the one there on the corner with the FOR RENT sign?"

She followed Drew's gaze. "That house. Oh, that's the old Creasey place. Isn't it awful? No one lives there now. In fact there's a neighborhood committee to get it condemned and torn down. My mother's the chairman," she added proudly.

"Well congratulations and all that," Pop said.

"But how can we get a look at it? I mean now. Without going back to Broadway and hunting down this Mr. Creasey."

The fat girl looked at Drew and then slyly shifted her eyes to me. "Well, it's locked—I guess . . . I mean, it's still private property. But if someone could crawl through a window. Well, of course, I couldn't—uh, that is, I wouldn't. But sometimes some of the neighborhood kids do, the smaller kids, that is . . ."

It took only a few minutes for me to crawl through the living-room window, walk across the creaky dusty floorboards of the big empty living room, and open the front door to Drew and the girl.

"What's it like, baby? Okay?" Pop brushed past me eagerly. He had a sense for these things—and besides he'd already seen the big yard that surrounded the place. I guess he knew that this was going to be the house.

The fat girl remained standing in the doorway, but I could tell from the way she didn't seem much interested in looking around that she'd been in the house before.

"It would be great to have somebody like you move into the neighborhood," she said slowly, eyeing me in a funny way. "But you wouldn't be thinking of moving in *here*, would you?"

"Oh, I don't know," I said, trying to sound cool about it all. "It's possible."

The girl exploded into a burst of laughter, although something about that laugh had a nasty ring to it, too.

"Listen," she said, sidling up to me in a confidential manner. "Nobody would move in here. This place is a dump. The last people that lived here were so awful they got run out of town."

"Why?"

She grinned and tossed her head. "Never mind. I don't tell neighborhood gossip."

"Then you shouldn't have mentioned it in the first place."

"Listen," the fat girl said, breathing heavily as she got even closer and went into a husky whisper. "The only kind of people who would ever rent or buy this place now is coloreds. That's why my mother and these other neighbors have this committee. Get it?"

I got it all right. But all I could see as I nodded dumbly was Inez' face when she heard about this. Mom would be livid. She might even throw things. There were some things she could get pretty sore about and one of them was prejudice.

For a minute I was tempted to tell the fat girl that my Mom was part American Indian and, therefore, so was I. And that was "colored," wasn't it? But I decided not to say anything about it just then.

"Look," I told her. "It's up to my folks, whatever my Mom and Pop decide. They might just take the place. They've got their reasons." Then I decided to get even with her for what she said earlier. "I can't say anymore, though. I don't tell family secrets."

She looked a little stunned but I could tell she caught on. For a second or two we just stood there glaring at one another.

Then, all of a sudden, she broke out into a big picture-window smile. "Well," she said, real warmly, "if you do move in here, I just know we'd be friends, huh? And I guess your folks would fix up the place so nobody'd ever even recognize it after a month or two." She paused. "Oh, I s'pose I should introduce myself. I'm Glenda. Who are you?"

And that—as I guess you guessed already—is how I met Fat Glenda.

3

THAT very same afternoon Drew and Inez and I drove to downtown Havenhurst to look up Mr. Calvin Creasey and see about renting the house. Of course, before that we had to drive back to "the box," as Inez called the apartment, and pick her up and take *her* to see the house.

At first she couldn't believe it. But after we got there and I crawled in the living-room window again and unlocked the front door, Mom was really excited. She rushed all over the place from the basement to the third-floor attic.

"You know," she said in a confidential whisper to Pop and me, after she calmed down a little, "it's spooky, absolutely spooky, to find a place as perfect as this."

Of course, anybody else's mother would have screamed at how awful the kitchen was and would have had a fit about the rusty plumbing and the cracked tile in the bathroom. There *were* plenty of rooms, though. About ten or eleven, I guess, if you counted all the little funny-shaped ones, including the round one that was shaped like a sharpened pencil point and stuck up at the top of the house.

After Mom finished looking around, Pop took her outside and showed her the yard and outlined some of his plans for where he would reassemble the two most important junk sculptures he had transported from California, and where he would pile his "raw materials."

They seemed to have everything figured out, and I only hoped they wouldn't be disappointed when they went to see about renting the house. Drew must have been a little worried, too, because he kept warning Inez not to appear "too anxious" when they saw Mr. Creasey; that might make Mr. C. up the rent.

The thing that kept bothering me the most was that, even thought it was a nice sunny afternoon and there were houses all up and down the street, not a single person came in sight the whole time we were there. Anybody would have known we were looking at the house for the second time that day because of the garbage truck parked out in front. Yet nobody showed up, not even Glenda.

All the way to Mr. Creasey's office, Inez kept humming and eating raw mushrooms from the bagful she'd gathered that morning on her bicycle trip to the woods. Every other mushroom out of the bag, she popped into Drew's mouth while he drove. Luckily, I had just had a chance to slap an L-burger together when we went home to get Inez and I was eating that now, cold. I know I said I couldn't go on with the alphabet-burgers after sharing K-burgers with Toby at our last meal together, but I guess the prospect of having a friend again had cheered me up, and anyhow the L was sitting around handy at the moment.

Finding Mr. Creasey took a little while. We got to the old business section in Havenhurst all right and found 108 Broadway. It was an upstairs office over a hardware store that still had advertisements for barnyard feed in the window and rolls of chicken-coop wire for sale out front.

The stairway up to Mr. Creasey's office was so dusty that our shoes left prints on the steps. At the top, the sign lettered on the door said that Mr. Creasey was a lawyer, realtor, county clerk, insurance agent, tax consultant, private detective, and notary public.

Drew turned the knob, which squeaked as though it was hurting. The door opened with a groan and we all walked in. Mr. Creasey was nowhere in sight, nor was anybody else. There was a big desk with papers and ledgers on it, all covered with dust, and some old chairs with cracked leather seats and oatmeal-colored stuffing peeking out. In the corner there was a long row of dark green metal filing cabinets, standing about six feet high.

While Drew talked in an unnaturally loud voice to try to attract someone's attention, Inez stalked around the office looking for cobwebs. Not that Inez was finicky about things like that or ever did "white glove" tests in other people's houses—not

29

Inez. No, it was just that Mom really loved cobwebs and she knew right away that this was a good place to hunt for some. Back in California, she had never let anybody brush away cobwebs or even kill spiders for that matter.

"Because cobwebs are nature's original designs and can give you the most wonderful ideas," she had once explained. "Like snowflakes, no two are ever alike." When she found a cobweb, she would draw its patterns on a piece of paper and put it away for her designs in hand-blocking or batik-making or weaving or whatever she was excited about at the moment.

Now Mom was crouching down, her eyes level with the top of Mr. Creasey's desk (she had spotted a terrific cobweb that looped across from one of the big ledgers to the top of an inkwell) when there was a sharp, crunching noise from behind the file cabinets.

Drew stiffened and said, "Mr. Creasey?" in an extremely loud voice. It was the kind of voice a person uses when he thinks there are burglars in the house and hopes there aren't. I just stood there with my knees turning to jelly and my fingers to ice. I didn't know if Drew or Inez had seen it but, along the tops of the file cabinets, I distinctly saw something very peculiar and very much alive bobbing up and down, and slowly moving toward us. . . .

A second later, a man stepped out from behind

the file cabinets. He was tall with sloping shoulders, a long wrinkled white face, ash-colored hair, and horn-rimmed eyeglasses. On his head he wore a dark-green eyeshade, like a baseball cap with no top.

"Sorry to have kept you waiting so long," he said in a deep mellow voice, as though it was the most natural thing in the world to step into a room from behind a row of filing cabinets. "Won't you all sit down. I am afraid I was occupied down below. You know what it's like to try to get a shop assistant these days."

I was relieved that he hadn't been hiding behind those cabinets the whole time we were there. There must have been a staircase, directly behind the file cabinets, leading up from the hardware store to the office.

Pop and Mr. Creasey (it *was* Mr. Creasey) introduced themselves to each other, and Mr. Creasey sat down at his desk, reached under it for a moment, and came up with a dusty gray rag with which he began to flick at the papers and ledgers on top.

Inez leaped forward. "Oh don't do *that*."

Mr. Creasey looked up startled. The lenses of his glasses caught whatever light there was in the room, and you could see how thick they were.

"You've got some lovely cobwebs there. I was just about to sketch one of them."

Mr. Creasey cleared his throat, nodded, and put

the dust rag away. "Yes, of course," he said, as though that, too, was one of the most natural things in the world.

"Now," he said, clasping his hands on the edge of his desk so as not to disturb any of the dust or spider webs, "how may I be of service to you?"

Drew came right to the point. "We want to lease that house you have up 'for sale or rent' here in Havenhurst."

Mr. Creasey cleared his throat again. "Ah, which house would that be?"

I suddenly realized we didn't even know the name of the street it was on and I couldn't remember seeing a number on the front door at all.

"Why, the gray clapboard one with the turret," Inez said, as though Mr. Creasey should have known that all along and not be asking silly questions.

"Ah," Mr. Creasey said, and leaned back in his chair.

Everybody sat silently waiting for somebody else to speak. Even Inez sat back and stopped sketching the cobweb. I really couldn't stand it anymore. I kept thinking of Glenda and of school starting in less than a week, and somehow I kept seeing Glenda's house with the picture window and the carefully tipped venetian blinds. I just had to get settled.

"Could you tell us what the rent would be?" I heard myself saying. Mr. Creasey dipped his head sharply in my direction as though he was surprised to learn I had a voice at all.

There was another long silence. Then, turning his lens on me so that once again they caught the light and gave him that blind but all-seeing look, he said, "My dear young lady, you don't really want that house."

Mom and Pop leaned forward and opened their mouths to speak. "But we do," I said quickly. "We do. I know it's pretty dilapidated, but it's the perfect house for us, because you see . . ."

Pop interrupted and I realized I was doing what he had warned Mom not to do. I was being too anxious.

"Is the house for rent or is it not?" Drew wanted to know.

Some more throat-clearing and Mr. Creasey said in his mellowest tones yet, "It is, of course. Yes, it is. But only for certain purposes. For ordinary domestic use, you understand. We can't have any more of that spiritualist activity there. No, oh dear, no. No séances, no table-rapping, no crystal-gazing, or fortune-telling."

"Séances!" Inez exclaimed. "Spiritualism? Whatever gave you that idea? What in the world could you be thinking of?"

Mr. Creasey pulled off his glasses and rubbed his eyes. "Why, excuse me if I am wrong. But aren't you?"

"Aren't we what?"

"Why, spiritualists, mediums, communicators with the spirits of the dead, fortune-casters. Or astrologers, perhaps."

"No," Drew said. "I don't think you understand at all. I'm a professor of social anthropology and I'm also an archaeologist. I've got a year's teaching contract at the State University College at Mill River. As I explained before, this is my wife and this is my daughter, Sara. Our son—he's sixteen—is living, for the time, with friends back in California. My wife here is just, uh . . . just an . . . ordinary housewife . . . with a few, uh, interesting hobbies. None of them have anything at all to do with the spirits of the dead . . ."

"I'm awfully curious," Inez said, leaning forward. "What made you think we were spiritualists, Mr. Creasey?"

Mr. Creasey put his glasses back on and ran his fingers across the brim of his green eyeshade. "Well, ah, to be frank, your appearance. It *is* a trifle unconventional. Oh, not for the college over at Mill River, I admit. But that's a good fifteen miles from here. Havenhurst is a very, ah, conservative community, as you have no doubt observed. They like things to stay just so over here."

Inez kept her eyes fastened on Mr. Creasey as he spoke. I wondered if she'd noticed Glenda's house or any of the others as we drove through Havenhurst. Some of them were big like Glenda's, but nearly all of them were what Inez would call "boxes."

"And then there's another point," Mr. Creasey went on. "They're all very house-proud people here in Havenhurst. Now, I'm willing to lease this house to you at a very nominal sum, but I'm not prepared to make any improvements in the property. It rents as is and I must tell you honestly that it requires a good deal of work. . . ."

"Oh, that's quite all right," Inez said with a faint smile. "We have plans for it."

"Ah, do you? Well, that's good. That's very good. I'm relieved to hear it."

Since I knew Inez' and Drew's plans better than Mr. Creasey did, I interrupted again. "What other houses have you got for rent around here, Mr. Creasey?"

Mr. Creasey looked surprised and leaned back with his hands clasped at the edge of the desk again. He blinked behind his lenses. "Other houses?"

"Yes."

"There are no others."

"Oh, I thought you said . . ."

"Never mind, Sara," Pop said. "This is the one we want."

Just looking for any excuse to keep us from moving into a whole lot of trouble, I said, "But what about the spirits of the dead. Maybe there are still some hanging around. Maybe on that winding stairway up to that pointy room at the top . . ." The minute I said that, I realized my mistake. Inez and Drew looked at me sharply.

Mr. Creasey gasped gently. "Then you've been inside the house," he said. But he didn't seem really angry about that. "Never mind," he went on, "I know that the neighborhood children often frolic about the place and have discovered a means of access."

I began to realize that Mr. Creasey was really much kinder than he looked. I decided to ask him another question.

"Is it because of the spiritualists who used to live there that the people in the neighborhood wanted to get the house torn down?"

Mr. Creasey seemed to know all about this, too. "That's what they've said. Of course, it did give the area an undesirable tone, having people come there for séances and readings all the time. In a way, I suppose you can't really blame them for having— ah—coerced Madame Cecilia and the others to remove themselves from the neighborhood. There is a town edict, you know, prohibiting anyone from operating a commercial enterprise in that section of town."

"Madame Cecilia?" I asked.

"Yes, that was the lady's name. She was the leader of the spiritualist group."

"What's this about the neighbors wanting the house torn down?" Inez interrupted.

I told Mom what Glenda had told Drew and me, and about Glenda's mother being chairman of the committee. But I didn't say anything about what Glenda had told me later on, about the fear of "coloreds" moving in.

Mr. Creasey rose. "Never fear, dear lady. Condemnation proceedings have not yet begun. It will take the better part of a year to accomplish anything of that nature and by then, I am sure, your neighbors will be so delighted with your demonstrations of good will and your improvements to the house that they will banish all such thoughts.

"Of course, as I have said," Mr. Creasey continued, "I can offer very little in the way of improvements to the property. But, as to the rent, I would suggest the following sum. . . ." Drew and Mr. Creasey were walking toward the office door now, and I heard Mr. Creasey mutter something to Drew. I saw Pop nod in agreement almost immediately. So the question of the rent seemed to be okay.

"Oh dear, I'm forgetting all about the keys. You'll want those, won't you?" Mr. Creasey hurried back to his desk and rummaged in one of the top drawers. After a while he came up with a bunch of very large keys, all covered with splotches of rust.

"Here we are," he said happily. He spread them out like the spokes of a wheel in the palm of his hand. "Front door, back door, side door, porch door, cellar door, hatch door, shed door . . . Or perhaps it's the other way around. I'm afraid I've quite forgotten. Oh well, you'll sort them out in due time, I'm sure."

Drew put the keys in the pocket of his blue denim jacket.

"Move in any time you like," Mr. Creasey said cheerily. "You can drop the rent in here or at the shop," he pointed directly below, "at the first of the month. Good luck."

We had been back in the truck about five minutes when I clapped my hand to my forehead and Inez and Drew both looked at me.

"What's up, baby?" Pop asked.

"The number, the address. Of the house. We still don't know it. I wanted to write a letter to Toby right away, tonight, and to some of my friends back home."

Inez snapped her fingers. "That's easy," she said. "Let's go and look."

We hadn't gone much out of the way yet. Drew turned the truck around and we headed for the house, just sort of following our noses like when we'd brought Inez to see it.

As we drove into the street, it seemed even quieter than before. It was about four o'clock in the afternoon now and you'd expect a *few* kids to be out playing. But no one. I decided it must be one of those blocks with nothing but middle-aged people living on it. That was probably why Glenda

38

was lonely and seemed anxious to have a friend in the neighborhood. And thinking of Glenda, where was she anyway?

We stopped in front of the house. The street sign on the corner said Dangerfield Road. So that was the name of the street anyhow. But what was the number of the house? I jumped down from the truck and went slowly up the walk toward the front door. The weeds on both sides of the cracked pavement were so long they tickled my ankles.

There was a small square porch at the entrance. It had wooden posts to support it and an arched wooden top. But there was no house number on the posts, on the arch above them, or on the front door. Then something else caught my eye. It was a small bundle of black and white fur nestled up against the front door.

A kitten for sure. I dashed up the three steps to the little porch. Nice, I thought. Nice to find a kitten waiting for you at the door.

I got up to it and kneeled down. Right away I realized it wasn't a kitten at all. It was more of a cat, only curled up in a funny way. I reached down to stroke it, but my hand stopped in mid-air. I knew why, too. Something was all wrong. It was a cat all right. But it was dead.

"Very amusing, I'm sure." It was Inez' voice, crackling with sarcasm. She was standing just behind me. "I wonder if they're trying to tell us something."

Drew was standing there, too. "No, I. It's just a neighborhood prank, I'm sure." Pop reached down, picked the poor cat up, and wrapped it in a piece of burlap from the truck.

I stood up feeling funny in the pit of my stomach. Who could have done it? And why?

Mom put her arm around me. "Don't brood about it, Sara. Oh, by the way, we spotted the house number."

"Where?"

"On the step."

As we walked to the truck, I looked back. There it was, very scuffed and faded-looking, on the riser of the middle porch step. Number 13.

So now we knew the full address of the house. It was certainly an odd address for a town that had such a cosy, homey-sounding name as Havenhurst . . . 13 Dangerfield Road.

P.S. I guess you're dying to know what L-burgers are.

S. M.

Well, even if you're not, I'll tell you anyway, because right now I need all the friends I can get. Limburger-burgers. Honest. Once you get past the smell, the taste isn't bad at all.

4

TWO DAYS later, we moved in. Glenda was there all right, watching the unloading of the garbage truck. Her eyes were ordinarily kind of narrow and slitlike because her cheeks were so chubby. But that day they were really popping.

"Is that your Mom?" she asked, when Inez got down from the truck and started lugging her zithers and harps and lyres into the house. I just nodded casually.

"I guess she's dressed like that on account of it's moving day."

"No," I said, just as coolly as before, "she always dresses like that."

I had been trying to cut the grass in the front yard with a squeaky old lawn mower that Drew and I found in the shed the day before. But it was no good at all. So now I was cutting it, practically blade by blade, with a hand clipper that was like a scissors held sideways, also very rusty and squeaky. Glenda was just sitting there on a big rock watching me and chewing on a 16-inch blade of grass.

"*My* Mom's too fat to wear tight pants and leotards and things like that. Although once, believe it or not, she tried to." Glenda spluttered into an explosion of laughter at the memory. "She went to this exercise class, see. And she bought a pair of black tights and a top. Only she didn't get them big enough because she was on a crash diet at the time and she figured she'd be losing weight real fast. And you know what? She split 'em! Right in the class, right in the middle of the exercise lesson. Oh boy, was she ever mad. She came home and ate a whole pint of cherry-cheesecake ice cream, just for spite. Say, ever try that? There's a place around here that has all those great flavors. Mmmm, they're yummy. I could go for a supercone right now. This grass tastes rotten."

Since Glenda herself had brought up the subject of weight, I figured it was okay to say something about it. "You ought to exercise more yourself, Glenda. Even this grass-cutting, crawling around on all fours—it burns up calories, you know. Better than sitting."

Glenda looked doubtful. "We have a gardener who comes around to take care of our place," she said. "My Mom gets palpitations if she works out in the garden, and my father has to watch his back or it goes out of whack. You ought to get one, too. A gardener, I mean."

"Drew's going to get a scythe and chop all this down. Then it'll be much easier to mow," I said.

"Yeah, but it's still going to look all scraggly. No one's lived here for over a year, and the people who lived here before never took care of the yard. It's terribly neglected.

"What were they like?"

"Who?"

"The spiritualists. That Madame Cecilia."

"Oh, then you know about them?"

"Of course. Mr. Creasey told us all about it. How come they got run out of the neighborhood? Were they really so awful?"

"Well sure. You should have seen what they looked like. Well, Madame Cecilia wasn't so bad except she dressed kind of funny and had this crazy way of talking. But some of the others—wow. One of them was an Indian. Supposed to be a swami or something. From India. Black hair, real dark skin. You know. He moved in after Madame Cecilia had been here awhile. He used to help her with her spook sessions. And then there were a couple of gypsies who moved in with her, both of them dirty-looking. They could hardly speak English. Don't know where they came from."

"I don't know," I said slowly, "it sounds kind of fun to me." Glenda was still sitting on her rock and I was crawling around her in a widening circle, snipping away to make a flat place in the grass. "In the town where we lived in California there were all kinds of people—Mexican, Chinese, Japanese. . . ."

Glenda sniffed. "My mother says California is for kooks. She says she wouldn't live there."

"Do you believe everything your mother says? I mean you never really saw California, did you? And even if she was right, what's so bad about kooks? Does everybody have to be the same?"

Glenda tossed away the blade of grass she was chewing on. She looked out past the front yard and past the picket fence, squinting hard, as though maybe she'd find the answer to my question out there. I followed her glance but there was nothing out in the street except three little girls, about eight or nine years old, wheeling fancy doll carriages and wearing their mothers' high-heeled shoes.

"Listen," Glenda said, suddenly leaning forward on her rock so that her legs just about came bursting through the husky-size light-blue denim jeans she was wearing, "you ask too many questions. I gotta think about all that stuff. All I know is, my Mom was real good to Madame Cecilia when she first moved in. My Mom used to come over here and chat with her. Sometimes she brought a pot of soup. Madame Cecilia was awfully skinny. She didn't do much food-shopping or cooking. She used to say her spirits brought her food."

"I thought your Mom and the other neighbors didn't like Madame Cecilia because she was running a business in the neighborhood."

Glenda looked confused. "Well, they didn't. But it wasn't so bad in the beginning. It was only after those weirdos began moving in with her."

"You mean if somebody was running a business

like a dressmaker's or an undertaker's or something like that in the neighborhood it would be okay just as long as they didn't have any dirty-looking people who couldn't speak English working for them?"

"Oh crumb," Glenda shrilled, pulling her fingers through her crinkly yellow hair in exasperation. "How should I know? There's probably some law against that, too."

I got up on my knees and pushed the hair out of my eyes. Between the grass clippings and trying to talk some kind of sense to Glenda, I was getting pretty tired.

"Well," I said, "I think it was kind of mean to kick the poor old lady out. I like gypsies and all that stuff."

Glenda grunted. "Well, you wouldn't like 'em living next door to you."

She got up from the rock and pulled the bottoms of her jeans down to her ankles. They had crept up and caught around her calves while she was sitting. Then she smoothed her shirt down over her stomach. She was always arranging her clothes like that. What a mountain of jelly! In spite of all the stupid things she'd been saying, I couldn't help feeling sorry for her. Anyhow, you could see she didn't really know any better. She was just rebroadcasting everything she'd heard her mother say.

"Listen," Glenda said, "I'm getting hungry. How about you coming over to my house for lunch? Think your Mom would let you?"

Let me? Glenda didn't know my Mom. I jumped inside the house, hoping Glenda wouldn't follow me.

Inez was setting up her harpsichord in the dining room. The living-room floor was full of those big pots she used for batiking and linen-dyeing and such. There was a den off the living room, and I could see Inez' and Drew's bedrolls and a couple of knapsacks dumped in there. I guess that's where they had decided they would sleep. My air mattress was probably upstairs in one of the bedrooms. At least, I hoped that was where it was. (My family never slept in beds because they were so heavy and clumsy to lug around.)

I kept looking behind me, just to make sure Glenda hadn't decided to trail me into the house after all, while I told Inez I was going over to Glenda's for lunch.

"Fine," Inez said, wincing at the same time because of a sour twang from one of the keys she was fingering on the harpsichord. "Drew and I are having wheat germ and black grapes and Roquefort cheese for lunch. You probably wouldn't care for that. Have a good time."

Glenda's house was just the way I'd expected it to be inside. It had rugs and lamps, tables and chairs, wallpaper and window drapes. The beds were in the bedrooms and the food was in the kitchen. And what food! The kitchen table, set into

46

a dining nook, had a great big shiny chocolate cake sitting on it. I thought I'd just about go out of my mind.

Meantime, Glenda was at the refrigerator bringing out bread and butter and mayonnaise and lettuce and sliced tomatoes and pickles and milk. From somewhere else, she got a big bowl of potato chips and a platter of crisp fried bacon.

"See, I thought we'd have bacon-and-tomato sandwiches. You like those?"

"Mmmm, do I."

"My Mom's not home. She's at a luncheon. She goes to a luncheon just about every other day. That's why she has this weight problem. But she can't help it, see. Because she belongs to all these clubs and organizations, and she's on all these committees. She knows about a million people. Boy, you can never get us on the phone because she's always on it. Talk, talk, talk. My father says she talks enough for both of them. That's why he doesn't talk much.

"My Mom made the cake. We'll have some for dessert. It's from a mix but she adds things and fixes it up so it tastes like real homemade. She won't tell anyone the secret. Not anyone. She fried the bacon for my lunch before she left and said it was all right if I asked you over."

I eyed the platter of bacon. It was enough for about six sandwiches—and not the kind you get at the 5-and-10 lunch counter, either.

"Of course, my Mom'll be dropping in at your house to say hello and meet your folks, maybe in a day or two. She thought it would be better to let them get settled a little first. But she's real friendly. You'll see. I'll bet she'll be inviting your Mom over for cake and coffee first thing."

All this time, Glenda was busy making toast and slicing pickles and tearing off chunks of lettuce. When it came to preparing something to eat, you couldn't accuse her of not getting plenty of exercise.

"How do you like our house?" she asked, crunching a mouthful of potato chips.

"It's great," I said, peering into the dining room and beyond that to the living room. In many ways it reminded me of Aunt Minna's except that it was much bigger. And although Aunt Minna had a lot of old things, all very neat and clean of course, everything in Glenda's house seemed new and shiny and expensive.

"It's so . . . planned out," I said. "Everything matches. I mean, it all goes together."

"That's because my Mom had it done by an interior decorator. You know, one of those ladies who always keep their hats on. Of course, my Mom didn't follow *everything* she said. A lot of it was her own idea, too. That's so there'd be some . . . individuality."

By this time, we were wolfing down the first of the sandwiches. Glenda made them so thick that slices of tomato came squooshing out from between the slices of toast and, while you were pushing them back in, strips of bacon came shooting out from the other side.

"These really are good," I said. "They're even better than alphabet-burgers."

Glenda actually stopped eating and looked at me in astonishment. "Than what?"

"Alphabet-burgers. Oh, you wouldn't know what they are. Nobody does. Because Toby and I invented them a couple of months ago. They never existed before that."

"Who's Toby?" Glenda pounced.

"My brother Toby."

"I didn't know you had a brother. Little or big?"

"Sixteen, going on seventeen."

Glenda smiled slyly. "Well, what do you know about that! But, wait a minute. Where is he? Hey, he's not in reform school or something like that?"

"Of course not! What an idea."

"Oh well, I'm just asking. I didn't mean anything bad. See, I know a kid from around here who nearly went to reform school. Same age. He goes to Havenhurst High. I bet you wouldn't believe that, from this kind of a neighborhood and all."

I told Glenda about Toby staying in California with the Gonzaga family so he could finish school there, but I could see she thought it was a peculiar arrangement.

"What's he like, anyway? Is he cute?"

"Very." I could see Glenda was interested, so I rubbed it in good about how terrific-looking Toby was and how independent and how we always had a thousand girls hanging around our house in California just waiting to get a look at him and hoping he'd take notice of them.

"Hmmm. I hope I get to meet him one of these days." Glenda was taking a breather between sandwiches, leaning forward with her elbows on the table and her knuckles curled up against her temples and a dreamy expression on her face. "So what about these alphabet-burgers that you two invented?"

I told her the whole story, but leaving out the stuff about Inez' and Drew's raw-food kick and all the other diets they'd been on. Then I told her what A-burgers and B-burgers stood for, and said she should try to guess the rest we had invented up to L. C was easy, of course, but she got stuck on D. I knew she would. So I told her I'd let her be a partner, starting with M-burgers, if she guessed five of the ten letters from C to L. She already had C, so she only needed four more. Without Toby around I sure could use another person to share alphabet-burgers with. And who was there to choose from, aside from Glenda?

Glenda was still trying to guess D when the front doorbell rang. "Come with me," she said. "It's probably somebody selling something."

We went to the living room, and Glenda tried to

peek out the window first to see who was there. There didn't seem to be anyone so she opened the door wide to look out. The next thing we knew something came flying into the room, something big and white that swirled over our heads in a loop exactly as though it was alive.

"What is that thing? Get it!" Glenda shrieked. The front door was still wide open and outside I thought I heard the sound of boys' voices laughing and hooting.

Glenda made a wild leap to catch the flying, white whatever-it-was as it nosedived toward an end table with a lamp and a lot of small china and glass knickknacks on it. As Glenda and I both swooped toward the lamp, my foot caught in one of the table legs which turned outward. Glenda tripped over my foot, and the next minute there was a terrific thud followed immediately by an awful crash!

I had managed to pull away and catch my balance just in time. But Glenda hadn't. She, the lamp table, and knickknacks were all in a terrible tangle on the floor. And everything seemed to be broken. Everything, that is, except Glenda. Suddenly a head appeared in the doorway. He was a kid, about our age, with light brown hair and eyeglasses and a laugh like a braying donkey.

Glenda looked up in a blaze of recognition. "Roddy Fenton!" she screeched. "I'll kill you! I'll brain you! So help me, I'll break your head!" To my amazement, Glenda scrambled to her feet in an instant and rushed out of the house. I watched her from the doorway, puffing her way down the street after him, still screaming, "I'll brain you, Roddy Fenton! I'll kill you. . . . I will, I will! So help me!"

I stood there in Glenda's mother's decorator-decorated living room and wondered what to do. There was so much broken stuff all over, I felt like somebody waiting for the ambulance to arrive and afraid to touch the wounded in case of doing more damage.

Suddenly my eye fell on the white "thing" that had come soaring into the room. It was lying among the broken bric-a-brac. I reached down and picked it up and saw that it was nothing but a paper airplane, but a very cleverly constructed one. I began to unfold it to see how it was made and I realized there was writing in it.

At first the printed-out words didn't make sense. Then they did. They were in verse form and here's what they said:

To the new girl. . . .
> Somebody fat
> Killed a cat.
> You'll find out
> She's a rat.
> WATCH OUT!

I was still standing there in Glenda's living room, holding the note in my hand, when I heard

Glenda's feet scraping tiredly up the front steps. I folded up the paper plane very small and pushed it deep down into the pocket of my dungarees.

Glenda staggered into the living room and flopped down in one of the soft plushy chairs. She was beet-red and dripping with sweat.

I sat down opposite her.

"Did you catch him?"

"Of course not."

She began rubbing her fists into her eyes. At first I thought she was just rubbing them and then I saw she was crying. She was a terrible sight. I was pretty upset about the note and what it said, but still I went over to her and offered her a wrinkled-up tissue from my shirt pocket.

She shook her head and took out a lavender-colored one, neatly folded, from her own pocket. She began wiping her face hard with it, trying to make out that the whole thing was sweat instead of a mixture of sweat and tears, like it really was.

"Gee, what a mess," she said after awhile, looking across at the toppled-over end table. "I shouldn't even be sitting here. I'll get this chair all damp and filthy. My mother'll have a fit. Oh boy, that lamp's broken for sure. What are we going to do?"

"I'm sorry I got in your way, Glenda. I guess I made you fall."

"Oh, it doesn't matter," she said miserably. "I'd have probably broken the stuff anyway."

The message in the note was really bothering me

but I couldn't bring myself right then and there to ask Glenda if she'd been the one to leave the dead cat on our doorstep. Was Glenda a sneak? Or was Roddy Fenton a liar? How could I tell? I didn't know him at all—and I didn't even know Glenda very well.

"What's this kid Roddy Fenton like?" I asked her, as we carefully picked up pieces and tried to put things back as close as we could to the way they had been.

"Oh, I don't want to talk about him," she said, lowering her head over the debris.

"Well, has he been living in the neighborhood a long time?" I asked hesitantly.

"Oh yeah. Since always. Look," she said, raising her head—I could see she was even redder than before. "This kid's a troublemaker. He's made a lot of trouble for me. He turned all the kids around here against me. That's why I've got no friends in this neigh—" She stopped abruptly. "What was that thing he threw in here anyway?"

"Oh, nothing," I said, "just a paper airplane."

"The dumb idiot."

After that we went back in the kitchen and Glenda cut the chocolate cake. She had two big pieces and I had one and a half.

"Listen," she said after awhile, "I'm not supposed to open the door to people if I don't see who they are first. So don't say anything to my mother about Roddy Fenton being here at all, huh?"

"Okay," I said, "but what *are* you going to tell her about how all this mess happened?"

"Oh, I don't know," Glenda said, "I'll think of something. But whatever happens, we'll stick together, huh? Like Monday, with school starting and all, I'll call for you and we'll go together. We'll really stick together. These other kids around here, oh, some of them are okay. But actually, well . . . really, to tell you the truth, most of them give me a pain."

Glenda took another big bite of chocolate cake. But right after that she put her head down and she made a funny choking sound in her throat. Maybe she had too much cake in her mouth. I couldn't tell. So I said, "Thanks, Glenda, really thanks a lot for the lunch. It was great. But I think I have to go now. I promised to help my Mom around the house this afternoon."

"Yeah," she said, without looking up. "Bye now."

I was just *sure* she was crying again.

5

I WAS pretty busy over the weekend, but on Monday morning, bright and early, Glenda was waiting for me on the corner so that we could walk to school together. It was nice strolling along under the big leafy trees, sort of like Crestview.

The school was new, a junior high school that had just been built the year before. I'd only seen it once, the week before when Drew took me over there to get me registered. All the way to school Glenda kept talking about the dream she'd had the night before.

"I dreamed the school burned down. It was so real, Sara. You know all that yellow brick? Well it melted. Like butter. The school turned out to be nothing but a big pool of dirty melted butter."

"That's crazy," I said. "A school like that couldn't burn down. It's probably the most fireproof building in all of Crestview—um, Havenhurst, I mean."

Glenda looked at me oddly but she didn't say anything.

As soon as we got near the school Glenda started waving to people she knew. Later she explained that they'd all been sixth-graders together at the elementary school she had gone to until last June.

"That's Mary Lou Blenheim," Glenda said, after calling out "Hi" to a tall girl with a pasty face and long straight hair that was so blonde it was practically white. "She moved here last year. Her family comes from down South."

Just then we piled into a whole group of girls who knew Glenda. They seemed so friendly I wondered why Glenda said all the kids in the neighborhood were "against" her.

"Hi Glenda. Did you have a good summer? Who's your friend?" There were two of them who always seemed to speak together. One of them, it turned out later, was named Cathanne and the other one was named Patty.

Glenda's eyes were really sparkling. "This is Sara," she said, "my friend from California. She's living here now, just a couple of doors away from me. Isn't that great?"

Another girl came over to talk and so did a couple of small runty boys. They were probably twelve or thirteen, but why were boys always so small for their age? Glenda repeated the same information to them. I kept wondering why she was telling everyone I was her "friend from California." It made it sound as though we'd been friends for years and years. And then I realized that was exactly how Glenda wanted it to sound.

Suddenly Cathanne, who had long red hair and

a nose with a very sharp point, got up very close to Glenda's face and squinted. "You're not supposed to wear lipstick to school, you know. You want to catch it the very first day?"

Glenda looked stricken and everybody's eyes became riveted to her lips. They *were* kind of cherry-colored now that I looked at them more carefully. Also, it seemed to me that her eyebrows looked different. They were sort of arched, and dark-looking, instead of golden-brown. And there were little brownish tails at the outer ends of them that curled up slightly.

But I didn't say a word. Poor Glenda. She was so fat. Her whole middle bulged as though she'd first wriggled into three or four bicycle tires that had been pumped full of air and *then* pulled her blouse and navy blue jumper on over that. I knew she thought about boys a lot and she wanted to look nice because there were plenty of boys— older ones, too—at this new school.

"It's not lipstick," Glenda protested, her cheeks getting nearly as red as her lips. "It's just that I've been biting them."

Six pairs of eyes stared at her.

"Well," she went on, "everybody's a little nervous the first day of school."

Cathanne and Patty looked at each other and grinned. "Oh well, it's your funeral. But don't expect them to believe that when they put you on a charge for wearing make-up." They turned and ran off laughing. The rest of the kids drifted after them.

As Glenda and I walked through the schoolyard on our way into the building, I saw Glenda wiping hard at her lips with one of those little lavender-colored tissues she always kept in her pocket.

Glenda was disappointed when it turned out that even though she and I had the same home-room and the same math and English classes, we didn't have the same lunch hour. I didn't mind so much because I figured it would give me a chance to meet some of the other kids at school.

Sure enough, Mary Lou Blenheim who was also in our homeroom asked me to have lunch with her the very first day. I could tell Glenda didn't like it.

"Did you really eat lunch with Mary Lou?" Glenda asked when we met in our eighth-period English class. "How'd you like her?"

"She seems very nice. I'm surprised you're not more friendly with her." Actually I'd only spent about ten minutes of the whole lunch period with Mary Lou because we lost each other in the first-day confusion of the school cafeteria, and I'd only found her again toward the end of the period.

Glenda bent over to reach for something under her seat. She came up red-faced. "She's with . . . with a different crowd. I don't think you ought to get too friendly with her, Sara. I can't say too much about it."

Oh no, I thought to myself, another one of Glenda's little mysteries.

On the way to school on Tuesday, Glenda said, "Don't worry about having to eat lunch with Mary Lou, Sara. I decided I'll go see my grade adviser today and I'll get my lunch period changed to yours. It only means they'll have to put me in a different French class."

"I'm not worried about it. If you do get your lunch period changed, then we could all three eat together. I don't think it would be nice to ditch her."

"Oh," Glenda said airily, "don't ever worry about her. She's got lots of other friends."

At lunchtime, Mary Lou and I went to the cafeteria together. This time things seemed a lot better organized and we chose places at one end of a long table near the entrance. Mary Lou had been telling me that she was a fussy eater and she always brough her lunch from home.

"Sometimes my Mom gives me watercress sandwiches and sometimes I get cucumber, sliced *very* thin with just a *shaving* of butter on the bread. I like things to be delicate like that, don't you?"

"Oh, I don't know," I said. "Sometimes I get real hungry at lunchtime. I think I'll go over and see what they've got at the steam table."

"I'll come with you," Mary Lou drawled, "just to get my cocoa. My Mom says I've got to have one thing hot. Oh, I just pray it isn't scummy. I hate that, don't you?"

"Oh sure," I nodded, half-turning to Mary Lou in the crowd that was beginning to collect for the lunch trays. We'd left our books and Mary Lou's lunch bag on the table to hold our places. "Everybody does. Hate scummy cocoa, I mean."

They had all sorts of crispy fried things at the counter and lots of roasted meats and stews all sloshing around in thick brown gravy. It just made my eyes pop and my mouth water. I figured if I could eat enough of that stuff every day at lunchtime I wouldn't even mind having a cold apple and a piece of sour-tasting cheese for supper. I finally made up my mind what to choose and got something called Hungarian goulash, with corn and French fried potatoes on the side. The lady who took my money at the cash register shook her head and said, "Too starchy."

On the way back to the table there were so many kids milling around I nearly tipped my tray bumping into one of them. It was a boy, brown-haired, wearing glasses, and with a funny sort of grin on his face. He looked familiar, but at first I couldn't place where I'd seen him before.

"Oh, 'scuse me," he said. "Hey, let me take that for you. Where are you sitting?"

I pointed with my chin to the table straight ahead where Mary Lou had already sat down with her cocoa. He put the tray down and, with that funny grin still on his face, he said. "Hi, Mary Lou." Then, before I could thank him he was gone, walking fast and slithering between the tables like somebody in one of those walking races where you're not allowed to run.

"I guess you know him," I said, sitting down next to Mary Lou.

"Oh sure, everybody does. His name's Roddy Fenton. He's all right but he's tricky. Know what I mean?"

I wasn't surprised when Mary Lou said his name. Of course—it was the same face I'd seen for a second at Glenda's front door after the airplane zoomed into the room. I wondered if I should say anything about that to Mary Lou and right away I decided not to. When you're new in town, it's better to ask questions than to tell tales.

I dug into the food on my tray. Mary Lou was still stirring her cocoa and hadn't even opened her lunch bag yet. "If I stop stirring it, it'll get scummy," she whined. "I just know it will."

I kept on eating. The Hungarian goulash was awfully good.

"Don't you find that stew kind of fatty?" Mary Lou wanted to know. "I'd be sure there'd be little bitty pieces of fat clinging to all those pieces of meat. So hard to see them, too, with all the potatoes and carrots and gravy and everything."

"What if there are? Fat's not poison, you know."

"Ugh," Mary Lou said, shuddering. She looked

at me a moment. "I'm surprised you're not fat, eating the way you do." She lowered her voice. "Like Glenda Waite. My, she's *really* a fat pudding, isn't she? By the way, she was here just a little while ago and she gave me a message to give you. Something about she's seeing her grade adviser at three o'clock, so don't wait for her after school. Said she couldn't stay to see you because she was late for her French class."

"Glenda was here?"

"Um-hmmm. Like I said, just for a minute. I found her standing here when I got back to the table with my cocoa. She said she recognized your red sweater hanging over the chair and my books on the table. I always cover my books with flower-sprigged paper because I think it's so pretty. Are you two really old friends from California?"

"Well no, not exactly. I only met her last week." I couldn't help thinking how fast everything had been happening lately. "I only just moved here to Havenhurst last week."

With her long, thin fingers, Mary Lou started to untwist the top of the paper bag that had her sandwich in it. "Oh, I see," she said slowly. "Then I guess you don't know her very well, do you?"

"No, I guess not. I guess I don't know anybody around here very well yet."

Mary Lou nodded her head with an air of great wisdom. "Um-hmmm. That's right. Oh well, you'll find out."

She sounded so mysterious that I couldn't resist asking, "Find out what?"

Mary Lou reached one hand into the paper bag, waving her head around slowly so that her straight white-blonde hair fell like a curtain of satin fringe. Her eyelashes, too, I noticed were very very pale, almost white.

"You'll find out," she said, "that Glenda's a squealer." I must have looked puzzled because she repeated, "That's what I said, a squealer. Now, you know, if there's one thing people don't like it's somebody . . ."

Mary Lou had just drawn her sandwich out of the bag. "Why, that's funny," she said, staring at the sandwich that was still wrapped in wax paper. "She never put lettuce on my sandwich before. She knows I hate it when it gets all soft and slimy. And why ever's this sandwich so fat?"

I was really beginning to get fed up with Mary Lou. I'd already finished every single thing on my plate *and* my two chocolate-covered doughnuts *and* my glass of milk. And Mary Lou was still stirring her cocoa, which had probably gone stone cold, and hadn't even opened her silly old watercress sandwich yet. Glenda might be a "fat pudding" and maybe even a "squealer," whatever that was supposed to mean, but I certainly preferred eating with her.

"Mary Lou," I said, "it's nearly the end of the lunch period." Lots of kids had already left the cafeteria. "Why don't you open that sandwich and eat it and get it over with?"

"I will," she said determinedly. She started unfolding the wax paper as though she really meant business. Then she stopped and stared at the unwrapped sandwich some more. Finally she took hold of the edge of the top slice of bread and started to tip it up to see what was inside.

I was so disgusted with her I put my elbow on the table and rested the side of my head in my hand while I looked as far away as I could, across to the other side of the lunchroom.

All of a sudden I heard a scream like an exploding siren coming from just behind my left ear. Right on top of this there was a terrible clatter followed by a crash.

I turned around to see Mary Lou's chair lying on the floor. Mary Lou herself must have jumped up from her seat and was already ten feet away holding her head between her hands and still letting out a sound like a police siren. Kids were all over the place trying to find out what the excitement was about. One of them even jumped up on the table where we'd been eating.

Then I looked down at the table and right beside me I saw Mary Lou's sandwich where she had left it. The top slice of bread was knocked off it and so were the lettuce leaves. And there, on the bottom slice of bread, they lay. Two scaly, yellow, raw chicken feet, side by side, the little clawlike toes covered with creased crackly skin and strewn with bits of feathers.

I looked up. The teacher who was on lunchroom duty had her arm around Mary Lou's shoulders and was leading her, still sputtering hysterically, toward the exit. The teacher tapped me on the shoulder. "You come too, please. Bring her books along and her sweater." She glanced down at the chicken-foot sandwich. "Oh, that's just too disgusting. I wonder who could have played such a mean trick?"

I wondered, too.

Roddy had shown up in the cafeteria during lunchtime. And Mary Lou had said he was "tricky." Then another thought came to me. Glenda had also been in the cafeteria during lunchtime, even though I hadn't seen her, and Glenda hadn't liked my having lunch with Mary Lou. Could Glenda have been the one who put the chicken-foot sandwich in Mary Lou's lunch bag? What a thought!

It was all too confusing and too difficult to try to figure out just then. So I picked up Mary Lou's things and my own, and followed Mary Lou and the teacher out of the cafeteria through the crowd of staring and whispering school kids.

6

AFTER school that afternoon I was helping Inez paint the big upstairs bedroom when the doorbell rang.

"Sara love," Inez said, from the third rung of the stepladder, "see who that is and tell them we don't want any. I've simply got to finish this ceiling today."

I went downstairs and saw a plump, smiling woman standing on the other side of the long, narrow window beside the front door. She was rapping on the glass with her knuckles and calling out in a loud musical voice, "Yoo-hoo. Anybody home?" Her other arm was curled around a big crimson cooking pot with a cover on it.

"Hello dear," she shouted, when she saw me approach the door. "Open up. I'm Mrs. Waite."

She didn't have to tell me. I knew right away that she could only be Glenda's mother and nobody else.

I opened the door and Mrs. Waite charged in, sort of breathless, and then stopped short and began looking around.

"Is your mother home, dear?"

"Yes, she is," I said. "She's upstairs painting the bedroom. I'll go get her."

"I hope I haven't interrupted anything," Mrs. Waite called after me. "Just wanted to say hello. And welcome to the neighborhood." I could see her moving around in the living room, looking for a place to set the pot down.

"You better come right down," I whispered to Inez the minute I got inside the bedroom. "It's Mrs. Waite, Glenda's mother. You know, I told you. . . ."

"Oh drat," Inez said, climbing down from the ladder. "I was hoping it wouldn't come to this." She stopped to peek into the bathroom mirror, and I watched her rearrange some of the clumps of hair that fringed her face. Then she gave a vigorous tug to the brightly dyed scarf she had tied around the rest of her long black hair.

Inez was dressed pretty much as she had been on moving day, in old black leotards (these even had holes at the knee) and a loose, short sleeveless smock of hand-dyed cotton in green, orange, and purple. Just for comparison, there was Mrs. Waite standing at the bottom of the stairs with her short honey-blonde hair frozen into stiffly sprayed waves and curlicues, and wearing a bulging strawberry-pink afternoon dress, nylon stockings, and tight shoes the color of vanilla ice cream. I hung back near the top of the stairs expecting that there just had to be an explosion when these two met.

"I guess I must have come to call too soon," I heard Mrs. Waite saying. "I see your furniture hasn't arrived yet."

By now I figured she'd taken in the array of dyeing vats on the living-room floor, the broken harpsichord and other dilapidated musical instruments in the dining room, and the bedrolls in the downstairs den.

"Oh yes it has," Inez said lightly. "It's all here."

There was a deafening silence.

"Well," Mrs. Waite said loudly and cheerily after a moment or two had passed, "I brought you a pot of nice homemade beef stew." I had reached the bottom of the stairs now and saw her extending the pot to Inez. "I cooked it this morning, early, because I had to go out to a luncheon. Otherwise I'd have brought it over sooner. I hope you haven't cooked your dinner for tonight yet. I thought it would come in handy with all the work you must have to do around this house. It's my own family's very favorite recipe."

Inez took the pot from Mrs. Waite and stood there dumbly.

I said, as hastily as I could, "Oh thanks, Mrs. Waite, thanks awfully. I just love beef stew. I'll bet it's delicious."

Mrs. Waite looked at me approvingly. "Everybody loves my beef stew," she said loftily. "But I'm afraid I'll need that pot back. If you could just put the stew into something else. . . ."

Still in a sort of daze, Inez went toward the kitchen with the pot of stew, mumbling something about going to look for a plastic container.

There wasn't any place to sit down in the living room except on the straw matting on the floor where Mom and Pop usually sat—and I'm sure that didn't occur to Mrs. Waite. So she remained standing and I could see she was sort of uncomfortable. But I didn't know what to suggest. Mrs. Waite wasn't as fat as her daughter Glenda, but then nobody was. She was kind of bulgy and lumbering, though, with a spare tire around her middle, and I could see why she'd gone to that exercise class and been on a crash diet and all.

"It looks as if your mother and father still have quite a lot of furniture to buy for this house," Mrs. Waite commented. She glanced around her in dismay. "It's a pity what they pay college professors these days. It's no wonder they have to take on an extra business on the side. Still—oh, I don't mean to get personal, of course—I just keep wondering how profitable that junk-collecting business of your father's can be."

Immediately there was a loud crash from the kitchen and Mrs. Waite jumped.

"It's nothing," Inez called out sweetly. "I'm just washing out your pot, Mrs. Waite."

"Oh, by the way," Mrs. Waite said, lowering her voice and looking at me intently with her pale blue eyes. "You mustn't think I came over here to tattle to your mother about that little mishap you and Glenda had in my living room last Friday when you came over for lunch."

"Mishap?"

"I know how it is when girls of your age get together," Mrs. Waite said. "You were just having fun and I'm sure you never intended to turn over a table full of pretty little glass and china pieces, and damage a valuable lamp."

I didn't know what to say. Had Glenda told her the accident was my fault?

Mom saved me by coming back into the room at that moment with the washed-out stewpot. "Actually Drew and I only eat foods that are as close as possible to their raw or natural state," Inez said briskly, as she handed back the pot, "so beef stew would be quite out of the question for us." She turned to me. "But I know Sara here will enjoy it."

Mrs. Waite's eyes narrowed. "Oh, I see. Then you're on some kind of health-food diet? So that's why you're so slim. Well, my dear, I do admire your figure. Still, a person's got to have a cooked meal once in a while. . . ."

"Not really," Inez broke in. "I don't think you'll find any scientific evidence to support that idea."

"Well, I'd go on your diet in a minute if I thought it would really help my weight problem. But," Mrs. Waite said playfully, "I don't think you're telling me the whole story. I've seen you out on that bicycle of yours, my dear, bringing home the groceries and so forth."

"Oh, have you?"

"Yes. But I suppose that's only temporary. Just until you get a car."

Inez shook her head. "No. The truck works out very well for general transportation and for hauling Drew's . . . stuff. I think we'll hang on to it."

I stifled a gasp. It was clear that Mom was heading for an all-out war with Mrs. Waite. And I couldn't do a single thing to stop her.

"Hang on to the truck?" Mrs. Waite asked.

"Um-hmmm," Inez nodded.

"That garbage truck?"

"Yes. Why not?"

"Oh, well really. I . . . I must go." Mrs. Waite's eyes scanned the living room. "I hope you get settled soon. Be sure to let me know if there's anything I can do. I'm always very busy. But still I try to be a good neighbor.

"You know," she said, shifting the red stewpot from one arm to the other, "it's funny, come to think of it. The people who've lived in this house have always been so . . . so different. Take Madame Cecilia, for example, the former tenant here. I tried to be a good neighbor to her, too. I often came over to bring her some of my good cooking— and I must say she *always* appreciated that. Of course, I didn't believe any of that spiritualist nonsense of hers. In fact, I think it may have unsettled her mind in the end. She began to make some very odd friends, you know."

Inez looked blank. "Oh?"

"Yes. She even took them in to live with her, here in this house. That's going a bit far, don't you think?"

"I really couldn't say. I don't know anything about it."

"That's true. You don't. By the way, I understand you're painting the bedroom. Is it Madame Cecilia's room, the master bedroom, the one she always used? Because I just loved the color scheme in there—those cornflower-blue walls with those royal-blue velvet drapes. . . ."

"Yes, it's that room I'm painting," Inez said.

"I suppose you're changing it to suit your own taste, yours and the professor's. But let me say this. If you should need any advice, any advice at all about decorating, I've got this marvelous decorator. . . ."

Mrs. Waite was really going too far this time. Didn't she ever know when to stop?"

"I've already decided on the color scheme for that room," Inez said impatiently. "It's going to be black and white."

There was a moment of silence.

"Oh dear, that sounds very . . . how would you put it . . . artistic? I'm afraid I can't picture it at all."

"It's, ah . . . different," I put in hastily.

"Yes," Mrs. Waite said, "I quite agree. Well, each to his own, I always say." She went to the door very quickly, calling out over her shoulder in a voice of mock cheeriness, "Good-bye now, I hope you're going to like it here."

The moment Mrs. Waite was out the door, Mom scampered upstairs without a word. She must have gone right back on the stepladder, picked up her paint brush, and started work. I had followed much more slowly and when I came to the door of the bedroom I just stood in the doorway, looking around and trying to imagine the expression on Mrs. Waite's face if she'd been standing there beside me.

Madame Cecilia's cornflower-blue walls had been painted a dead chalky white by Inez. But since there were big cracks and other uneven places in the plaster, Inez had hit on the ingenious idea of painting big fat squirming black arrows up the walls. Some of the arrows were thicker and wigglier than others. But they all pointed upward from the floor to the ceiling and ended with their tips touching the ceiling.

Right now, Inez was painting the ceiling itself.

"Do you really have to paint it that color?" I asked.

"Black's not a color," Inez said, without looking at me.

It was true all right. Inez was painting the bedroom ceiling black. Jet black. At first I'd thought her whole idea of painting the room was fun. Now I wasn't so sure.

"I don't think we made a very good impression on Mrs. Waite," I commented.

"I don't think she made a very good impression on us," Inez said, in an expressionless voice.

"She'd really think we were crazy if she could see this room."

Inez merely grunted.

"Well, don't you think it's sort of creepy? I mean, those squirming black arrows all around and that solid black ceiling."

Inez turned and stared at me in some surprise. "Oh come on, Sara. Where is it written that all bedrooms must be painted cornflower-blue?"

"Well, not cornflower-blue exactly. But isn't there something else—something in between? Oh, *you* know what I mean."

"Black's just right for a bedroom ceiling," Inez crooned softly as she slapped on another brushful of paint. "Couldn't be more appropriate. 'As black as a night without moon or stars; as black as a dreamless sleep.'"

I gave up and went back downstairs. There was no point in trying to talk to Inez when she got into one of her poetic moods.

Along about suppertime, Glenda phoned me. She sounded all excited.

"Listen, Sara, I had to wait until 4:30 to see my grade adviser. And I can't get my program changed until next week. They have to find a different French class for me. So I *still* can't have lunch with you. Isn't that disgusting!"

I didn't answer. Everything that had happened in the cafeteria came back in a rush.

"There is one good thing, though," Glenda went on. "Mary Lou Blenheim was in the office when I was there. She was getting permission to go home for lunch for the rest of the term. At least now you won't have to eat with *her* anymore."

"I guess you heard what happened to Mary Lou today," I said.

Glenda snickered. "Oh, sure. Everybody around school was talking about it."

"Well, *I* think it was awful, don't you?"

"Oh, yes. Of course, I didn't see it. But it must have been terrible when it happened. Those two raw chicken feet lying there on that slice of bread. Were you right next to her when she opened the sandwich?"

"Of course. Glenda," I said, slowly, "who do you think could have done it?" The suspicion that had come to my mind as I was leaving the cafeteria was really beginning to nag at me now.

There was a pause at the other end.

"Who knows? Anybody." Glenda lowered her voice and quickly changed the subject. "By the way, Sara, my mother told me she was over at your place this afternoon. What happened?"

"What do you mean 'what happened?' She brought over some beef stew. It looks good. In fact, I'm going to have it for dinner."

"No. Other things. About some things your Mom said."

"Like what?"

Glenda was whispering. "It's hard for me to talk right now."

"Oh, well in that case I'd like to ask you about some things *your* Mom said."

"Like what?"

"Like about the lamp that got broken over at your house on Friday," I said, more than slightly irritated. "Did you tell her I was to blame?"

"Oh Sara. Never! What made you think that?"

"Well, I know I *was* in a way. If I hadn't tripped you by accident. . . ."

"Uh-uh. I told her it was all my fault. I honestly did. In fact, I'm giving up three weeks of my allowance money to pay for having that lamp fixed. Sara, what kind of a friend do you think I am?"

That was a good question. What kind of friend was Glenda anyway? A jealous friend? A possessive friend? A sneaky friend? Or really a good friend?

"But you still didn't say what you told your mother about *how* it happened?"

"Oh . . ." Her voice dropped. "Like this . . . I

was showing you around the house and my arm accidentally brushed something off the table and then when I bent down to get it . . . you know."

"But why, Glenda? I know you said you weren't supposed to open the front door without looking, but you could have said you did look first and it was this boy you knew. I mean, it really was this kid Roddy's fault, so why should you take the blame for him?"

"Look Sara," Glenda said indignantly, "I don't squeal on people. Even on people like that. So forget it. It's okay. Really."

Funny. That was exactly what Mary Lou had called Glenda—a squealer.

I was anxious to know what Glenda meant about "some things" my mother had said to her mother. But we didn't have a chance to talk about that until Wednesday afternoon after school.

We were sitting on the front steps of our house. Glenda leaned confidentially toward me and said, "Well, when Mom came back from your house yesterday, I could tell her feelings were hurt."

"About what?"

"The beef stew she brought over. It seems your Mom told her right off that she and your Pop wouldn't be eating it."

"I know. But I ate it and it was great. I'll be sure to tell your Mom and thank her."

"Oh, she'll like that," Glenda said absently. "Another thing, though. She said your Mom acted kind of snippy. Did she?"

I sighed. "Well, Inez is like that sometimes. She doesn't mean anything by it. I guess she got upset because your Mom criticized a lot of things. Not directly. But in a sort of roundabout way. And I could tell it was annoying my Mom."

"Like what things?"

"Oh you know. The way the house is fixed up inside, the junk my Pop collects for his sculpture, the garbage truck. Your Mom even thought my Pop was in the junk-collecting business to make extra money because he wasn't getting paid enough at the college!" We both spluttered into laughter at that one. "She said it when my Mom was out of the room, but I know Inez heard it."

Glenda was shaking her head. "I guess maybe they won't be friends," she nudged me with her shoulder, "like us."

"I guess they won't."

"Well, don't worry about it, Sara. Your family may be different, but I like the way you call your Mom and Dad by their first names. And it really must be adventurous, sleeping on mats on the floor and all that. Almost like camping out, instead of having everything so stiff and . . . and arranged. Like we do."

I sat there thinking over what Glenda had just

said. I suppose she meant it. But she didn't have to live in my house.

"Camping out and all that is fine," I said. "But there comes a time, for me anyway, when I want to go *home*. So I'll be happy to change places with you any day, Glenda. You can come and live in my house and eat raw food and sit on the floor. And I'll go over to your place and take my chances on breaking lamps. Just think, if I were there I could be stuffing myself with chocolate cake made from secret recipes, beef stew, fried chicken, barbecued spareribs, and cherry-cheesecake ice cream!"

"That does it," Glenda exclaimed. "I'm getting hungry. It's nearly suppertime anyway so why don't we go over to my house and cook M-burgers. I'm dying to try them."

"Will it be okay?" I felt odd about going over there now that Glenda's mother was so upset about us Mayberrys. "I mean, with your mother not liking us very much."

"Oh no," Glenda said. "She likes *you* very much. Know what she said about you last night?"

"No. What?"

"She said you seemed so nice and normal she wonders what you're doing in that family."

Oh no, I groaned inwardly to myself.

"That sounds like Mrs. Hinkle," I said to Glenda.

"Who's Mrs. Hinkle?"

"Oh, just a lady. Well, our landlady in California if you want to know. She lives about three thousand miles away. But she and your Mom must have mental telepathy. Or something."

P.S. I guess you're wondering what Glenda and I finally decided on for M-burgers.

S. M.

Mozzarella-burgers. That's that Italian cheese. You put a slice on a grilled hamburger and stick the whole thing under the broiler until the cheese melts and oozes and gets all golden-brown. When you bite into it, the cheese stretches into long, skinny strings, like bubble gum. You'll like it.

7

IT BEGAN to be more and more noticeable that people in Havenhurst were talking about us.

One of the people I found this out from was Roddy Fenton. I saw Roddy around school, of course, but he usually kept at a distance, especially if Glenda was around. Then, two weeks after Mrs. Waite's visit, Glenda was absent for a couple of days.

"Hi," Roddy said, catching up with me as I was walking home from school on the second day of Glenda's absence. "Where's Fat?"

Before I could answer he leaned over and took a couple of heavy schoolbooks out of my arms. It felt lots better with just my notebook and a skinny math book left to carry.

I was annoyed with him for calling her "Fat," though, so instead of saying thanks, I said, "If you mean Glenda, she's sick. With a virus or something."

Roddy just loped along beside me looking straight ahead. "Oh, *too* bad."

"I don't think you really mean it."

He stopped short and stood in the middle of the sidewalk looking at me.

"Listen, if you two want to be friends, what do I care? In fact, you want to know the truth? I think you two make a real freaky pair. So go ahead and be friends for life." He started walking again, shaking his head as though he was agreeing with himself.

It was my turn to stop now. "Okay, give me back my books. You don't have to bother *acting* like a gentleman, carrying lunch trays and books around for me, because I don't think you *are* one."

Roddy pulled back. "Hold on a minute. Don't get sore. What'd I say that was so terrible?"

"Plenty. And the way you said it, too. So Glenda and I arc freaks, huh? What's that supposed to mean?"

"It means what it says. She's a freak. That's what. Fat as a house. Crazy, too. That kid's not normal. You just got to admit she's freaky."

"And me, too, I suppose?"

For the first time Roddy seemed uncomfortable. His face turned kind of pink.

"Well," I said, "I'm still waiting. What's freaky about me?"

"You?" he said blankly. "Uh . . . nothing. You look okay to me." He stopped and stood there rubbing his ear, then started walking again. "But, I'll tell you something. That family of yours. Wow!

Some kids and I passed your house the other day and this dame was out in the yard boiling something in a big pot. Looked like a witch. And there was this whole pile of junk sticking up in the middle of the yard, only it was all connected like it was supposed to *be* something."

The things Roddy was saying made me feel terrible. I kept walking along looking at the cracks in the sidewalk.

"Listen," he said, putting a hand on my arm. "It's not your fault. Lots of people have nuts in their families."

His trying to be kind about it made me angrier than anything else. "They're not nuts," I said hotly. "They're my parents and I love them. Now give me back my books and leave me alone!"

But Roddy just stood there holding onto my books as though I'd put him in a trance.

I glared at him. "Is that why somebody left a dead cat on our doorstep? Because they'd decided we were a bunch of nuts before we even moved in?"

He still didn't say anything.

"And then you threw that dumb note into Glenda's house."

Roddy half smiled. "Oh, so you read it?"

"*I* did. But Glenda didn't see it and I didn't show it to her. Incidentally, you ought to be grateful to Glenda. She never told her mother about your throwing that paper airplane into the living room."

"So what?"

"Well, a lot of stuff got broken because of it and Glenda got into a lot of trouble. It's costing her fifteen dollars in allowance money. But she took the blame. She told her mother it was all her fault because she didn't want to squeal on you."

"Big deal!" Roddy said bitterly. "She's a number one squealer from way back—and don't let anybody tell you different."

"Then why didn't she tell on you?"

"Oh," Roddy shrugged. "How should I know? Probably because you're a new friend and she wants to impress you with how noble she is."

"Then why would she have put that cat on my doorstep? You know what I'm beginning to think? I'm beginning to think *you* put it there, Roddy Fenton, to try to get Glenda into trouble."

Roddy whirled around in front of me. "Oh yeah? Prove it!"

That was the whole trouble; I couldn't prove anything. Even though I wanted to trust Glenda, I couldn't get the thought out of my mind that she had had something to do with Mary Lou's chicken-foot sandwich. And whoever had planted the chicken-foot sandwich might very well be the same person who had left the dead cat. So I was still wondering about Glenda—and I remembered that Mary Lou, too, had called her a squealer.

Roddy and I had started walking again, and we

were getting close to the corner of Dangerfield Road.

"You can give me back my books now," I said. "You might get scared by witches if you walked down my block."

Roddy handed me the books. "Listen, I'm sorry I made you mad or if I hurt your feelings or anything. But, number one, you want to watch out for Fat. She's not what you think she is. And, about your folks and that yard full of junk, I might as well tell you it's no joke. There's a petition going around. Somebody came over to our house with it last night, and my Pop signed it."

"A petition? What sort of petition?"

"Well, it's got something to do with your folks running a junk-collecting business. It says they gotta haul all that stuff out of the yard and get rid of that garbage truck."

I didn't want to believe him but his face was dead serious.

"That's not true, Roddy. They can't make us do that. We're not running a . . ."

"Sure they can. They can make you do anything around here if they once get after you. They can run you out of the neighborhood; they can put you in jail. Anything. Take it from me," he said, moving in closer. "I ought to know."

"What's that supposed to mean?"

"Look. Don't ask questions. I'm just telling you

what I know." He began to walk backwards slowly, down the street and away from me. "No joke."

It turned out that Roddy Fenton was telling the truth. On Sunday, Mr. Creasey showed up at our house, driving an old beat-up black Ford. Instead of his green eyeshade he was wearing a straw hat, even though it was already October and getting a little chilly. Mom and I were both in the house. We could see Pop and Mr. Creasey talking in the yard. Most of the time they just strolled around as they chatted, and Pop seemed to be showing his junk sculpture to Mr. Creasey. Once, Mr. Creasey even went up a few rungs on Drew's ladder to get a better look at the construction under progress. This stovepipe one was going to be a monster, about fourteen feet high, Drew said.

After about half an hour, Mr. Creasey left and Pop came inside.

"Did he come for the rent?" Inez asked matter-of-factly.

"No," Drew said. "I dropped that off a few days ago."

"He came on account of the petition, didn't he?" I blurted.

Inez and Drew both looked at me in surprise.

"Oh, so you knew about that," Pop said.

"I heard about it the other day. A kid from school told me."

"Why didn't you tell us?" Drew asked.

"I thought he was making it up," I said sheepishly. "At least, I hoped he was."

Drew outlined the petition for Inez while she listened to him wide-eyed.

"Of all the nonsense I ever heard," Mom exclaimed. "Did you explain about your sculpture, Drew?"

"Of course. You saw us out there. Creasey was as nice as could be about it. He was quite interested in 'Stovepipes,' too. Took a long look at it."

"So that's all settled then," Inez said.

"Well, I guess so. Creasey's on the town council. He says as long as we're not running a business enterprise, the other members can't register any official beef against us. Said he was delighted to learn it was just a hobby after all and that he was impressed with the 'vigor and originality' of my work."

"He's a dear fellow," Inez said absently. She was busy setting up her loom for a new weaving project.

"What about the garbage truck?" I asked. Even though I knew how calm Inez and Drew could be about things that got other people terribly upset, it was amazing to me that they didn't seem more uneasy and hurt about the petition. After all, it was a serious thing.

"What *about* the garbage truck?" Drew wanted to know.

"Can you go on keeping that in front of the house?"

"Well, actually Creasey said he couldn't see any technical objection to it as long as it isn't being used for commercial purposes."

"But it is awfully ugly," I said.

"It's also serviceable, Sara love, and it cost a song," Mom commented. "I've gotten to love that old load."

"Well everybody else around here just hates it!" I said. "Did you know that? Even you've got to admit it's pretty terrible-looking."

"Oh rubbish," Inez said impatiently.

Drew was staring out the window at the truck, which was parked as usual in front of the house. "I could rip down a section of fence and pull it into the yard under those trees," he said.

"Why should you?" Inez wanted to know.

"Oh, maybe just for Creasey's sake. He's being nice about things. And people *are* talking about it, I."

"Well of all the nerve . . ." Inez began.

"Nobody would say anything about *anything* we did if you just didn't make it so noticeable," I broke in.

"Noticeable? What's that supposed to mean?" Inez wanted to know.

"Oh Inez," I said imploringly, "can't you see that we're different from everybody else around here? I know we were like this in California, too. But there we weren't the only ones in the whole town. Here we really *are* different. People in Havenhurst are sort of old-fashioned and . . . well, straight. The same families have been living here for years. They don't have a lot of new people from all over the country moving in and out all the time and changing things around the way they do in California. Havenhurst is more like . . . well, like Crestview, Ohio. Like when I lived with Aunt Minna."

"Ah, I might have known it," Inez said exasperatedly. "Crestview and Aunt Minna."

"Hold on a minute, I," Drew said to Mom. He'd been intently watching us both. "Did you ever notice that you're about as antagonistic to Crestview and Aunt Minna as Havenhurst is to us? More, probably."

"Oh that's nonsense," Inez retorted.

"Pop's right," I said. "You are against them, and that's why they watch us and act so picky, though really the garbage truck and the junk in the yard *do* look awful. This is a pretty-looking street. Or it was until we moved in."

Inez just glared at me.

"Did you know," I went on, "that they ran Madame Cecilia out of the neighborhood, not just because she was running a business but because she took in an Indian and some gypsies to live with her? And did you know that the reason they wanted to get this house condemned and torn down was because they were afraid that . . . well, afraid that the only people who would move into a dump like this would be . . ."

Inez lifted her arm. "I know. Don't tell me. Do you think I can't spot racially prejudiced people from a million miles away? What are you trying to say Sara, that we must conform to Havenhurst and not be ourselves anymore? Haven't we taught you anything? Haven't you any convictions at all? Don't you even know what you believe in anymore?"

"Of course I do," I said angrily. "But I just don't think people around here are as ready for changes as they are in some other places. Glenda understands because I explain things to her all the time. But most people around here only judge us from the way we dress, or the way we take care of the house and the yard, or something like that."

It was awfully quiet in the room. Mom just sat there at her loom with her hands in her lap.

After a while Drew got up and went to the window again. "She's right, I," he said to Mom, without turning around. "I'll pull that truck in the yard. Easy enough. Make a gate out of the section of fence I take down. Maybe build a shed for the junk materials, too. Won't do them any good sitting out there with winter coming on."

I went over to the window and stood by Pop while he pointed out where he'd put the shed. "See, there along the side. Straighten the whole place up. Make it look more like a sculpture garden than a junkyard."

"Okay," I heard Mom say very quietly and slowly, from what seemed like very far behind us. "Okay, move the truck off the street and have a shed. But some things stay as they are. My black ceiling does, for one."

Inez' tone was brave but her voice sounded small. Like a little girl.

"Sure," I said. "That stays."

I turned around and went and put her pretty dark head against my chest. She felt surprisingly limp against me. It just broke my heart that Roddy Fenton had called her a witch, after he saw her out in the yard with her dye pots. If she was a witch, she was probably the most beautiful witch in the whole world.

8

A FEW weeks before Halloween something wonderful happened. We got a letter from Toby. It said:

"The Gonzagas are moving back to Mexico around the first of the year. They've asked me to come with them but I think I should finish high school in the U.S. So how about if I come East and pick up the school year there right away?"

How about that! Was I happy. Of course, Toby felt rotten about leaving Felipe because they were great friends and had spent a terrific summer on the archaeological dig in Mexico that their school had sponsored. Toby had a lot of questions about Havenhurst, but Glenda had even more questions about Toby.

"Does he have a girlfriend back in California? He's probably going to be the most popular boy in Havenhurst High. The girls there are all boy-crazy, you know. I wish I was in high school already, don't you? Is his hair much longer now than when you left California? Do you think he'll cut it before starting school here?"

"How do I know, Glen? When you meet him

you can ask him. It's only a few more days now and he'll be here."

"Oh gosh, am I really going to meet him!" And Glenda blushed a watermelon-pink.

On the day when Toby was scheduled to arrive, Drew borrowed a station wagon from one of the other instructors at the college. Even Inez agreed that driving the garbage truck all the way to Kennedy Airport and then grinding around the airport in it to pick up Toby at the terminal building was going to be a downright nuisance.

"I suppose we'll actually have to get rid of it one of these days," Mom sighed, as we set off for the airport.

The station wagon Drew had borrowed was pretty old and battered, but it felt like a magic carpet after the garbage truck. It didn't go very fast, though. And after we got to the airport we had to drive around on so many weaving and winding roads it felt as if we were going in complete circles. Then there was the long wait in the terminal building where Toby's flight was due.

But, at last came the announcement of the flight arrival and about ten breathless minutes later, there was Toby.

It wasn't really that long since I'd seen him. It was only that so much had happened since we left California in July. And now it was October—and

Toby looked different somehow. Much older, lots taller, and with a dark, reddish-brown sunburn.

His hair was longer, as Glenda had somehow suspected it would be, and fuller too. With his craggy features and dark, dark eyes, Toby looked even more like an American Indian than he really was (which wasn't much, considering how mixed-blooded even Inez' Indian relatives were).

Toby was excited and happy, moving around in tight little circles, grinning a lot, and with that mischievous glint in his eyes.

On the drive back to Havenhurst, Toby and I got sort of quiet. It was as if we had so much to say to one another that we couldn't think of *anything* to say. I couldn't get used to this new, handsomer, more grown-up Toby. I felt shy with him somehow.

"Got a lot of new girlfriends?" Toby wanted to know.

"No, not a lot. Just one, really. She *is* a lot, though." I giggled. I didn't mean to make fun of Glenda. I never did, not even in my mind. But suddenly I was seeing her through Toby's eyes. I knew Toby didn't like fat girls and I knew Glenda was going to be crazy about Toby. So I wished there was some way I could prepare him, so he'd like her just a little bit.

"What do you mean, she's a lot? Oh-oh, I think I know. Never mind."

"No really, Toby, she's awfully nice even though she is a little . . . well, overweight. Her name's

Glenda. And another thing, I hope you don't mind but she really is a pretty good friend to me, so I told her about alphabet-burgers."

"So?"

"Well, we've been eating them all along. Mostly we cook them over at her house. I know it was supposed to be a private thing between us—you and me. But I didn't know if you were ever coming East."

Toby leaned over and put an arm around my neck in a mock choke. That was more like old times.

"No, I don't mind, silly. Don't be so serious. It's okay, really. In fact, to tell you the truth, I forgot all about alphabet-burgers."

"Oh, you *would!*" I said, wriggling out from Toby's stranglehold. "Listen, it's a good thing you're here. You can help us figure out something for the letter Q."

"Q?"

"Yes. We're up to Q-burgers. The last time I saw you we were having K-burgers. Do you remember that?"

"Oh sure," Toby said. "Kraut-burgers. Who could forget them? Gee, how'd you get all the way to Q? Must have been an awful struggle."

"Well it was."

Just then Drew turned off the parkway and a few minutes later we were stopping in front of 13 Dangerfield Road.

"Hey, look at the yard full of junk construction," Toby exclaimed. "How about that."

"Watch your language, please," Inez said, clearing her throat. "Drew now calls it his 'sculpture garden.'"

Mom went on into the house, and Drew and Toby were so busy hauling Toby's gear out of the station wagon and commenting on the house that they didn't see Glenda hiding behind the big tree to the side of the porch steps. But I did.

As soon as Toby had looked over the inside of the house and decided to bunk up in the round, pointy-shaped turret room (I just knew he'd choose that one), I ran down and met Glenda in the yard.

"Oh my goodness," Glenda squealed, "he's gorgeous. I think he's the most gorgeous boy I ever saw. I just think he's stunning. You didn't tell me his hair was that long. Will he cut it or not? Oh I don't care what he does. When will I get to meet him? Could it be real soon? I mean, like right . . ."

"Glenda," I said, "stop talking. Stop it because I'm going crazy."

And I *was* going crazy because now that I'd taken a good look at Glenda I couldn't believe my eyes. I just stared at her and tried to figure out what she'd done to herself. Because this wasn't Glenda at all. It was somebody about twenty years old with gorgeous cherry-colored lips and creamy, slightly blushing cheeks, no freckles at all. And with deep mysterious eyes that had long black fringes on them.

Oh, of course, underneath it all, she was still Fat Glenda. She was wearing her bulging navy blue jumper that she had worn the first day of school, except it was shorter than I remembered it. A lot shorter. And high-heeled shoes the color of vanilla ice cream that I knew belonged to Mrs. Waite because I'd seen them on her myself.

Glenda smiled. "Well, how do I look? Say something."

"Glenda," I said, shrugging my shoulders, "you look wonderful and you look terrible. I mean . . . I don't know *what* to say. See, you're really very pretty, but it's sort of too much. And it isn't you."

Glenda lowered her eyes. "You mean you don't want to introduce me to Toby. I look too stupid."

"No you don't. You look very glamorous really. But . . . oh, how can I explain it? See Glen, Toby just got here and he's all excited. And he's changed a lot, Glenda. I think he's become very sophisticated. And if he saw you the way you look now he might think it was just . . . well, kid stuff. You know, a silly kid trying to *look* grown up."

Glenda just stared at me for a little while and then a great big muddy tear began to roll down one of her creamy-pink, no-freckles cheeks.

"Some friend," she said chokingly.

"Glenda, I am," I pleaded. "It's just that I think it would be better for you to meet Toby after he's more settled and calmed down. And not looking this way. As yourself."

She grabbed my arm. "But I don't *like* myself. I hate myself. He'll hate me too when he sees me as myself."

I was embarrassed for Glenda and I didn't know what to do. But then a thought came to me. Maybe Toby wouldn't notice how much make-up Glenda had on because he'd never seen her before. He didn't know the Glenda I knew, with her freckles and her light-brown golden-tipped eyelashes and her pale lips, and her whole face sort of hanging out and showing itself. He'd just think *this* was Glenda and maybe he'd think she was pretty. Because really she was.

"Know what," I said, after thinking about it a little more, "you're probably right. Why don't you come on in the house now and I'll introduce you."

"You will? Really?"

"Uh-huh."

"Oh good," she said, brightening at once and dabbing at her eyes with one of her little lavender tissues. "Oh Sara, I'm so excited. Only please don't walk too fast. These shoes pinch something terrible." I could hear her huffing and puffing behind me as we crossed the yard.

"I was planning on wearing my mother's wig, too," Glenda confided, as she panted up the front steps just behind me. "The blonde one that falls in a flip. But wouldn't you just know, of all times, she picked this week to send it out to the wig shop to be curled."

A wig was all Glenda needed.

9

FOR THE next few days Glenda did nothing but ask me questions about what sort of an impression she had made on Toby.

I had a hard time telling her. It wasn't that she had made a bad impression. In some ways, I suppose it was even worse than that. It was simply that she had made no impression at all.

After all the trouble she'd gone to, and all her excitement about meeting Toby, I didn't know how to tell her that about fifteen minutes after she left our house I mentioned her to Toby and he said, "Who?"

Of course Toby had been awfully busy at the time, stowing his things away in the turret room and calling down to Inez on the second floor, answering and asking questions about everything, like how were Inez' old friends in California and could he have a piece of galvanized pipe to use as a clothes rack (there was no closet in the turret room).

About a week after Toby's arrival we were having a pow-wow on the living-room floor—Inez, Drew, Toby, and me. That's what I always called them—pow-wows. Because we all sat around cross-legged on cushions, although Inez usually stretched out on her belly. I suppose other families have most of their talks and family conferences around the dining-room table. But since we didn't have a dining room *or* a table . . . well, you know the rest.

Toby had started school at Havenhurst High and he was already writing a column for the school newspaper. Also he was organizing something he called a "community-awareness" committee. It was supposed to keep the student body informed on neighborhood relations, civil rights violations, and things like that. Toby was telling us all about it.

"Perhaps, after your committee gets going," Drew suggested, "you might find out who it was who considered us such a menace in the neighborhood. It's not really important but I've often wondered who started that petition."

Toby had heard all about the petition and about Mr. Creasey's visit of warning. He grinned and shrugged. "Well, maybe. It's a little out of our line."

We were still talking about Toby's ideas for the "awareness" committee when the doorbell rang. I went to answer it. To my surprise it was Glenda. She didn't usually come around in the evening and besides she was hard to recognize at first because she was wearing a long, dark rain cape with a pointy hood on her head that came down nearly over her eyes. And it wasn't even raining out.

"Gee I'm glad you answered, Sara," she whispered. "Can you come here a minute?"

I closed the front door behind me and went out on the porch even though it was cold out there.

"What is it, Glenda? Why can't you come inside?"

She didn't say a word. Then with a broad sweep of her arms she flung open the cape and threw her head back so the hood fell off.

"Look! It's my Halloween costume. I'm rehearsing."

In the dim porch light I could see enough to make me gasp. This get-up was *really* something. Glenda had on all the make-up she'd used when she met Toby—and then some. Besides, she was wearing the long blonde wig that curled in a flip.

She also had on a long white robe made out of what looked like a couple of bedsheets that were tied around the middle with a glittery rhinestone belt. She lifted the hem of her skirt. High-heeled silver shoes with rhinestone buckles. She lowered her eyelids. Glitter dust that sparkled like diamond chips on their bulging surfaces.

Glenda continued to stand there. "Well?"

"Does your mother know you're wearing that wig?"

"No," Glenda said in a tense whisper. "And she's not supposed to find out. It only came back today from the wig shop. I told you, I'm just rehearsing this costume."

"So how do you expect to borrow the wig for Halloween?"

"Oh, don't worry," Glenda singsonged. "I will." She peered past me trying to see into the living room through the glass panes alongside the front door. "Is Toby home? I thought maybe he could give me his opinion on my costume. Do you realize it's only nine days to Halloween and you don't even have your costume decided yet? You are coming trick-or-treating with me, aren't you? I mean you've just got to, Sara. Friends always do."

I shivered. "It's cold out here. Come on inside, Glenda. Toby's here. So are Inez and Drew." She hung back a little. I knew she always felt shy and out of place with Mom and Pop even though she was always saying how much she really liked them. Well, I couldn't blame her for that. They certainly were different from the kinds of grown-ups Glenda was used to.

When we got inside, the living room was empty. Toby had gone up to his room, Drew was busy doing something in the den, and Inez had just gone into her workroom, which had big sliding wooden doors and was supposed to be used as a dining room.

So I had to take Glenda up to Toby's turret room again and this time I didn't see how he could help noticing her.

Well, we got up there and I pushed Glenda into

the open doorway of Toby's room and he noticed her all right. He jerked his head up from some stuff he was writing and said, "My God, what's *that?*" Glenda blushed awfully.

"No, wait a minute. Don't tell me. Let me guess."

Even though she was getting redder and redder, I could tell Glenda was enjoying this.

Toby went through all sorts of beginning guesses like, "it's . . . uh . . . oh no. No, it isn't that at all. It's . . . ah . . . no, it isn't really that either. Well, I would say that what it really is . . . is . . . is . . ."

Glenda turned around for him, making a full circle. But that didn't seem to help.

"What's that black thing you're carrying?" Toby wanted to know.

"Oh that's my rain cape. I wore it to come over here. It covers the whole thing. Even my head."

"Good," Toby said, half-seriously. "Tell you what. Why don't you just put that on and we'll all try to forget the whole thing."

"Oh come on, Toby," I said. "You're not being at all nice. This is Glenda's Halloween costume. She came over to show it to you. To get your opinion."

"Halloween? My opinion? Oh, come on girls. I'm kind of busy here."

"I know you are. But just say at least what you think of it."

"Well . . . it's okay, I guess. For Halloween."

Toby really looked into Glenda's face for the first time. "Who are you supposed to be anyway?"

Glenda began to turn hot pink again but she looked straight at him.

"Snow White."

"I see," Toby said. "That's very good. A fine choice of costume." He turned back to his writing and picked up his pencil. "And a very happy Halloween to you both."

It was pretty clear that Toby expected us to leave. But to my surprise Glenda stepped forward.

"It's nine days yet to Halloween, and Sara doesn't even know what her costume's going to be yet." She turned to me. "Do you, Sara?" I shook my head no. "But anyhow," Glenda went on, inclining her head toward Toby, "I wanted to ask you if you would come trick-or-treating with Sara and me on Halloween."

I was almost as surprised at Glenda's request as Toby was. He stared at her, open-mouthed, pointing to his chest with one finger, as if to say, "Me? Are you crazy?"

Glenda took a few more steps toward Toby's desk.

"See, let me explain. You could protect us. All the kids around here—except the real little ones—wait until after dark before they start trick-or-treating or collecting for UNICEF. They all wear masks and sometimes they play tricks on one another and

106

it can get pretty rough. Last year a girl got sprayed with green paint. And a lot of the kids throw eggs. You wouldn't have to wear a costume or even a mask unless you wanted to. You could just wait for us out on the sidewalk and walk us from house to house."

Toby raised his eyebrows. "Do you mean to say that you two are going to spend a whole evening going from house to house, ringing doorbells and yelling out 'trick or treat,' and collecting a whole lot of junky candy to eat? Aren't you both a little old for that?"

"No, we're not, Toby," I said, deciding it was time I helped Glenda out. "All the kids our age around here do it. Come on, Toby. Please say you'll come along with us. Even if you think it's nutty, it's the kind of thing big brothers are supposed to do. Say yes."

Toby scratched his head.

"Please?"

"How's about if I say 'maybe?' "

"How's about if you say 'maybe yes?' "

Toby nodded. "Okay. 'Maybe yes.' But remind me about it again a couple of days before, huh?"

Glenda squealed and grabbed me by the shoulders. She was so happy she said why didn't I come over to her house right now and we could talk about my costume and have Q-burgers and hot chocolates. Her mother and father were both out for the evening and she had to get back and put her mother's wig away, and also the silver shoes and rhinestone belt, before her mother got home.

It took a few more days but at last I had a great idea for a costume to wear on Halloween. It all came about because Glenda's mother had so many white bedsheets that she didn't want anymore. Mrs. Waite had just bought all new colored sheets for the beds to match the color schemes in her newly redecorated bedrooms.

It wasn't easy to think of something to do with white bedsheets that wouldn't be ordinary. Anybody could be a ghost or even a white witch. When I finally thought of what I would be, it was so simple.

I'd be the Statue of Liberty. I'd carry a flashlight for a Statue of Liberty torch (it would come in handy getting up the steps of some of the houses with lots of dark shrubbery where the people didn't leave porch lights on) and I'd make a crown out of cardboard, with spikes coming out of it in a sunburst pattern.

A couple of nights before Halloween, while I was in the middle of working on my Statue of Liberty crown, I got a telephone call. It turned out to be Mary Lou Blenheim.

Mary Lou was still going home for lunch every day but I saw her in classes and sometimes she phoned me about the history homework. We were only a little friendly because Glenda was around me so much of the time and stuck so close that I didn't really have a chance to talk much with any of the other kids—which was, of course, the way Glenda wanted it.

I thought Mary Lou's voice sounded funny, different from when she called about a homework assignment.

"Are you alone, Sara?"

I looked around me. "What do you mean, alone? My mother and father are around here somewhere, and my brother's upstairs in his turret . . . uh, in his room."

"Huh?"

"In his *room*."

"Oh, well that's okay I guess. I really meant do you have any friends there with you?"

"Like who?"

"Oh . . ." Mary Lou hesitated, "like Glenda Waite. Well I *know* she lives next door to you."

"Not *right* next door," I corrected her. "Anyhow she's not here. Why?"

"Well," Mary Lou lowered her voice. "Some of the kids got together and we decided to have a party on Halloween. After trick-or-treating. It isn't going to be at my house because of my grandmother being sick and staying with us. It's going to be at Roddy Fenton's."

Mary Lou paused as if she was waiting for it all to sink in.

"Hmmm," was all I could think of to say.

"Yes, that's right," Mary Lou went on. "Roddy has a big finished basement at his house. Well, anyhow, what he said I should ask you is could you come to the party? It's going to start about 9:30. After we trick-or-treat. There's no school the next day, but you can tell your mother the party will end about 11:30."

I knew Mary Lou was waiting for an answer but instead I couldn't help saying, "I didn't know you and Roddy were such good friends."

"Oh, *that*," Mary Lou said. "Sometimes we're not. Sometimes I could just kill him. Like I told you, he's tricky. He does lots of pranks. But we go around in the same crowd. More or less. And anyhow parties are fun. Can you come?"

"By the way," I said, still not answering Mary Lou's question, "did you ever find out who put that chicken-foot sandwich in your lunch bag, Mary Lou?"

"Eeek! How can you even mention that! Wasn't it *horrible?*"

"Yes, but did you ever find out who did it?"

Mary Lou giggled softly. "Oh, Roddy finally confessed to me that he did. Just for a prank. Because I was hanging around with you and you were a friend of . . . well, you know, of Glenda's."

What a relief! At last I knew it wasn't Glenda after all. Right away I felt guilty, thinking how I'd been suspecting her and not really trusting her all along. I could have kissed Mary Lou, I was so happy to hear it was Roddy.

"But aren't you even angry at him, Mary Lou?"

"Well, he explained about it. He didn't really mean it as a prank against me. He had certain reasons. But then Roddy does all sorts of pranks all the time, so you can't really take it too seriously. He's like that."

An idea came to me. "Does he leave dead cats around, too?"

"Dead cats?" Mary Lou sounded vague.

"Yes. Dead cats. Does he ever leave them around for a prank?"

"Well, actually," Mary Lou drawled, "now that you mention it, I heard he did that once, too. Isn't he just awful?"

I let out a sigh.

"Oh, he didn't kill it, mind you. He found it somewhere, run over by a car, I think. Still, I don't know how he could *bear* to pick the thing up. So listen, Sara, you still didn't say . . ."

"Mary Lou," I said hotly, "you're asking me to go to a party on Halloween and you know very well that Glenda is my friend and she and I are planning to go trick-or-treating together. In costumes and everything. We've got it all planned. . . ."

"Well, I know. But this is *after*."

"And Glenda isn't invited?"

"No," Mary Lou said softly, "she isn't." Neither of us said anything for a moment. "Well, it's at

Roddy's house like I told you. For myself, I wouldn't care all that much . . ."

"Never mind explaining, Mary Lou. Because if I were Glenda, I wouldn't go to that party even if Roddy got down on his knees and begged me. After all the rotten things he's done to her. . . ."

"Hold on a minute," Mary Lou said, getting a little ruffled. "What about the rotten things Glenda did to Roddy?"

"Like what?"

"Well, I heard some things. But I really don't think I should talk about it. It's none of my affair. It would be up to Roddy. Look, Sara, why don't I have Roddy phone you? It's all getting to be too much for me to puzzle out."

"He doesn't have to," I snapped. "If he had his reasons for not inviting her, he shouldn't have invited me either. It's just another way of hurting Glenda. He knows we're friends and I can't go without her. I'd be leaving her flat."

After I hung up I was so mixed up I couldn't think. Because in a way I would have liked to go to Roddy's party, even though I was furious at him now that I knew he had gone to such lengths to get Glenda in trouble. You see, I was beginning to realize I *could* have other friends in Havenhurst if it weren't for Glenda.

But the very next minute I was angry at myself for thinking that way. Glenda was a true friend, and she deserved my loyalty. I'd be ashamed to ever tell her about how I'd suspected her. But why did Roddy want to get Glenda into trouble? What *had* Glenda done to him?

Nobody wanted to talk about it. It was beginning to look as though I'd never find out. And Glenda and I would just go on together, keeping to ourselves and being . . . what was it Roddy had called us? . . . a freaky pair!

P.S. I guess you think it's impossible to invent an alphabet-burger starting with Q.

S. M.

Not really. Although it's next to impossible. But Glenda and I did it. Quack-burgers. Chinese duck sauce (the kind you put on barbecued spareribs) smeared on top of the hamburgers instead of ketchup. Very good.

10

THE DAY of Halloween was just perfect. Not a California Halloween, with flowering shrubs and palm trees on people's front lawns, but a real honest-to-goodness witches' Halloween with dry, crackling brown leaves all over the ground and just a few red and gold and yellow leaves still hanging on for dear life to the crooked black branches overhead. It was chilly out, too, with a swooshing wind that got stronger toward afternoon.

That morning at school, though, I had a shock. Mary Lou Blenheim passed me a note in homeroom. When the piece of folded paper reached me, I looked up and saw Mary Lou nodding her head to let me know it was from her and I should go ahead and read it. I immediately looked around for Glenda and saw that she was at the back of the room, tacking up some posters that Miss Ames, our teacher, had given her to put up.

So I opened the note quickly, holding it flat on my lap. It was written in block letters in red ink, on graph paper.

It said: "To Sara Mayberry—this is to invite *you and Glenda W.* to my party tonight—Halloween.

9:30. Use basement entrance and come in a costume. Be seeing you."

It was signed: "Roddy F." The words "you," "and," and "Glenda W." were underlined in black.

Well! The words really jolted me. Roddy Fenton certainly had a way of sending surprising notes to people. My first instinct was to write on it, *"No, thanks!,"* fold it up again, and pass it right back to Mary Lou.

When I glanced up, Mary Lou was smiling and still nodding and Glenda was just returning to her seat. I was about to shake my head from side to side to indicate "No" to Mary Lou, when I realized it wouldn't be right for me to refuse the invitation for Glenda without her knowing anything about it. I'd have to talk to Glenda, of course.

So instead I just sort of shrugged at Mary Lou as if to say, "How should I know?"

It was hard to concentrate during my math and history classes that morning. I knew I wouldn't have the chance to speak to Glenda until lunchtime. Even without her knowing how Roddy had tried to break up our friendship, first by trying to put the blame on her for the dead cat and then by inviting me to his party without her, I figured she'd definitely say no.

And of course I'd have to say no, too.

There was one thing that kept nagging at me, though. Even if Roddy was only inviting Glenda because he wanted me to come (which I guess he was), suppose I *did* get Glenda to go to the party? Mightn't that be a way of patching up the quarrel between Glenda and Roddy? Maybe everything would come out in the open at last. If they'd both done wrong and admitted it, then we could all be friends. And I'd be the one who brought them together.

Well, it was a nice thought, anyway.

Lunchtime finally came around, and I met Glenda in the cafeteria. I had to be careful how I told her about the invitation. I couldn't show her the note. The underlining in black made it look very fishy. So I said that Roddy had asked me in the school corridor between math and history classes.

At first Glenda turned very pale and let her mouth hang open. Then she just kept saying she couldn't believe it. After a while she started shaking her head and didn't say anything at all. Her lunch was getting cold in front of her and she wasn't even eating. Which wasn't at all like Glenda.

"I was sure you wouldn't want to go," I said. "Not after the way you feel about Roddy. So why don't you eat? Your chow mein is turning to glue right in front of you."

Glenda took a gulp of gluey chow mein and sticky rice, and right away she started to cough and sputter. "If only . . . I knew . . . *why* he asked us," she stammered, still coughing.

"Well, he asked us. That's all I know. I figured

you'd say no, but still I had to tell you about the invitation, didn't I?"

Glenda seemed to be thinking hard. "It's probably just a trick. You know, Sara. Halloween and all."

"Ummm. Probably." I didn't want to force Glenda into accepting because I still wasn't even sure of my own feelings. And trying to bring Glenda and Roddy together could easily bring on an explosion instead of what I had in mind.

"You don't think," Glenda said after awhile, "that Roddy could have found out . . . no, he couldn't have. And even if he did, he wouldn't care."

"Found out about what? Not care about what?"

"That time when he threw the airplane into the living room and I never even told on him."

"Oh that." I'd never talked to Glenda about my conversation with Roddy a few weeks back. He hadn't seemed impressed when I told him Glenda had protected him. But maybe, just maybe, that information *had* softened him toward her a little. Still, I doubted it.

"If I *had* told," Glenda said, "you can be sure my mother would have sent the bill for the lamp over to the Fentons. She does things like that."

"Look Glenda," I said, "maybe we should just forget about going to the party. We'll trick-or-treat and then we'll go over to your house or my house and eat the candy we collect."

Glenda took a few more mouthfuls and choked some more. Finally she asked, "What do you think they'll do at the party?"

"Oh, I don't know. I suppose it'll probably just be a bunch of noisy kids eating popcorn and ducking for apples. I don't even know where Roddy lives."

"It's not far," Glenda said quickly. "I wonder who's going to be there."

"He said Mary Lou for one."

"She's not too bad," Glenda said, looking more relaxed. "I sort of like Mary Lou, don't you?"

"I always said she was all right. You were the one who didn't seem to like her."

"No. She's okay. It's kind of funny about Mary Lou going, though," Glenda said. "I didn't want to say anything but I always thought it was Roddy who put the chicken-foot sandwich in Mary Lou's lunch bag."

I didn't say anything. I couldn't tell Glenda about my telephone conversation with Mary Lou. And besides I still felt guilty for having suspected Glenda of having done it.

"Well, I don't know," Glenda mumbled. "It might be fun."

"Roddy did say to come in our costumes. Glenda, imagine what they'd say if they saw you in that gorgeous blonde wig, and with the glitter-dust on your eyelids."

Glenda beamed and stared off into space, across

the noisy clatter of the school cafeteria. It was as though she wasn't thinking about herself at all but about somebody else, some distant and wonderful movie star.

Suddenly Glenda leaned across the table, nearly plopping her elbows into what was left of her chow mein. "Listen Sara, let's do it!"

"You really want to?" I said matter-of-factly, trying to sound surprised and not *too* pleased about it.

But, of course, I was pleased. I figured it was a chance for both me and Fat Glenda to break out of our tight little worlds. Maybe we weren't such a freaky pair after all!

When Glenda and I got home from school that afternoon, Toby was out in our yard working on "Stovepipes." Pop had been on it for weeks, and now it was nearly completed—all fourteen feet of it, the tallest junk structure Drew had ever designed. There was also a car parked out in the street in front of our house, one of those souped-up jobs that a lot of the kids from Havenhurst High went ripping and zooming and throbbing and chugging around the neighborhood in. But I couldn't see anybody around who might be the owner.

"Stovepipes" was the same construction that Mr. Creasey had admired when he came around early in October about that petition that was being circulated against us. It really was made of stovepipes, the big black ones that Drew had picked up in September when we'd been driving around in the garbage truck looking for a house to live in. Lots of other things had gone into it, too—from old tin cans to automobile fenders.

Toby was way up near the top fastening some screws and bolts, or whatever it was that held Pop's junk constructions together.

Glenda nudged me. "Does he know what time we're going trick-or-treating tonight?"

"Toby," I shouted. "We have to talk to you about tonight."

Toby looked down. "Oh, say, about that . . . sorry, kids. No can do."

Glenda made a face and looked at me.

I squinted up at him. "What do you mean? You said you'd come with us. Glenda and I were counting on it."

Toby shook his head. "I didn't promise. I only said 'maybe.' "

"You said 'maybe yes.' "

"There was still a 'maybe' in there somewhere."

"Toby," I said insistently, "can't you come down? I want to talk to you."

"In a minute." A few seconds later Toby began to wriggle down from the top of "Stovepipes." He jumped the final three or four feet to the ground. "What's up?"

"Well, it's just that I can't see how you can disappoint Glenda and me like this. What *are* you doing tonight anyway?"

Toby put a hand on my shoulder, as a sort of limp apology, I suppose. "Going to a party with some of the kids from school." Then he headed off across the yard toward the shed where Drew kept most of his junk piled.

I stamped my foot. "Oh, you're rotten!"

Toby turned around, wrinkling his brow and making flapping motions with his hands. "Take it easy. I'm sure you two can manage to go trick-or-treating on your own. Glenda's big and strong enough to protect both of you."

I turned to look at Glenda. She was staring after Toby and her eyes were stormy. And then an odd expression came over her face. For a second I thought she was going to scream something terrible at Toby, and the next second I thought maybe she was going to cry, and right after that she looked scared. All she said was something that sounded like "Oooh," and with that she turned and ran out of the yard.

I could have just killed Toby. Instead of following Glenda, I started toward the junk shed. Then I saw the other boy who was back there with Toby and whom Glenda must have seen, too, when she got that odd look on her face. But why?

He was tall and lean and very, very good-looking. About sixteen or seventeen, I guess, with a gorgeous fading-gold suntan, the kind that lifeguards have after being at the beach all summer, and with thick brown hair that swept down low on his forehead. It seemed odd that Glenda would have run away, with any boy that good-looking around. But of course she was terribly angry at Toby. And so was I.

"Listen," I said, going straight over to Toby and ignoring the other boy for the moment. "What did you mean by talking to Glenda like that? She's very sensitive about how big and fat she is. You're not supposed to refer to her size. Don't you realize you hurt her feelings?"

Toby looked surprised, which made me even angrier. "Did I? Okay, okay. I'm sorry."

"Sorry? Sorry's no good. You already said it."

"Okay, okay. I'll apologize," Toby said impatiently. "Oh, by the way, this is Bruce Fenton. Bruce, my sister Sara. Bruce is a pal of mine from school. He came over to scrounge around in the shed for some auto parts for his . . . hmmm, pardon the expression . . . vehicle. When I told him about some of the stuff Pop's been collecting, he nearly flipped."

"Hi," Bruce said. He had a perfect smile with a set of perfect, absolutely white teeth, which made his good looks so perfect it was almost blinding to look at him, and also it made me very uncomfortable.

"Oh," I faltered, "then I guess that's your car out front."

Bruce just grinned.

"Did Toby say your last name's Fenton? You

wouldn't by any chance know a boy named Roddy Fenton?"

"Nope. Never heard of him."

"Oh, I thought maybe . . ."

Bruce broke up into a falsetto laugh. I was glad to find out that at least there was one thing about him that wasn't perfect, because I thought boys with high-pitched laughs sounded just terrible.

"I was only kidding. Actually I do know the little guy," he said. "Matter of fact, he's my brother."

"I didn't even know Roddy had a brother . . . until now. Nobody ever mentioned it."

"Oh sure," Bruce said absently. He was holding up a couple of rusty, dented old hub caps that he seemed to be considering for the wheels of his car.

I could see Bruce and I were at the end of our conversation. And anyhow I still wanted to have it out with Toby about Glenda. "It's bad enough you broke your promise," I said, talking to Toby's back as he combed through the junk looking for something for Bruce, "but saying that to Glenda when you know she's my best friend. I think she ran out of here crying."

To my surprise it was Bruce who looked up. "Did I hear you say she's your best friend?"

"Yes, of course she is. Why shouldn't she be?"

Bruce glanced at Toby and then back to me. "I probably shouldn't get into this."

"No," I said. "I want to know what you meant

just now. Why shouldn't Glenda and I be best friends?"

Bruce's face began to redden a little under his fading tan. "Look, you got a right to be friends with anybody you like. It's just that personally I can't see being pals with somebody who's tried to make trouble for you?"

"What trouble?" Toby wanted to know.

"Didn't you people know there was a petition circulating to try to get you kicked out of the neighborhood?" Bruce looked around the yard. "On account of all this junk and that . . . that 'Stovepipe' or whatever you call it."

Bruce stopped to consider. "You know, I sort of like that thing, though. It gives me an idea. When I'm ready to junk my car and go for a new one, I'll make an artistic-looking monument out of the old one, and stick the whole thing on our front lawn. Let's see what old lady Waite'll do about that!"

"What's she got to do with it?" I asked.

"Oh boy," Bruce said. "How dumb can you be? Didn't you even know she was the one who started that petition against you? She cooked up the whole idea, calling people on the phone and getting them all worked up about it. Then she got a couple of *other* people to go door to door with it, getting folks to sign. But everybody around here knows it was her baby." Bruce paused and looked straight at me. "I'll bet that fat pal of yours never even told you."

I stood there with my mouth hanging open. "No. No, she never did." Then I thought I had the answer. "If Mrs. Waite did start the petition, I'm absolutely sure Glenda didn't know anything about it."

"You're sure, are you?" Toby challenged.

"Oh yes, Toby, I am."

I could see that Toby didn't believe Glenda was innocent.

"All right," I said, "I'll just go right in the house and phone Glenda and ask her. Is that okay with you?"

Toby and Bruce both looked at me. They didn't say anything. Then they turned away and started fishing around silently in the junk again.

The minute I heard Glenda's voice answering the telephone I knew she was very upset, but it was hard to tell about what or at whom.

"What's the matter?" I asked her.

"Nothing. Why'd you call?"

"Listen, Glen. Toby said he's sorry about what he said."

She didn't say anything. I went on. "I know that doesn't help much. He shouldn't have said it."

Still no answer.

"Well, listen Glenda, don't be angry at *me*. I didn't say it. Or is there something else you're angry about? Oh, come on, Glenda. It's not the

t time somebody said something rotten to you.
on't be so sensitive."

"Oh," she said sullenly, "what would *you* know
about it?"

"Plenty. I've been hit on the head, too, you
know. In fact, there's something I have to ask you
right now and please tell me the truth."

"I don't tell lies!" Glenda snapped.

"Okay. Calm down. I didn't say you did."

"You made it sound like I did. And I don't!"

"Okay, okay. What are you getting so steamed
up about? Glenda, *please,* just tell me this. There's
some kind of talk going around that it was your
mother who started the petition. You know, the
one that said how we'd have to get out of the
neighborhood."

"Who told you that?" she said suspiciously.

"Well, it really doesn't matter because everyone
around here seems to know and we only just found
out. So all I'm asking you is was it really your
mother who started it and, if it was, did you know
that she was doing it?"

It was dead quiet at the other end of the wire. I
could hear my heart pounding louder and louder.
But still no answer from Glenda.

"Glenda," I said hoarsely, "I asked you a question. You're supposed to be my friend and you said
you'd tell me the truth. So tell me, can't you?"

I didn't think she was ever going to answer me

and then her voice came over the wire, twisted and nasty. I'd never heard it like that before.

"You know what *I* think," Glenda snarled. "I think that from now on you'd better stick to *your* family and I'd better stick to *my* family!"

And, with that, she hung up on me.

11

INEZ and Drew were getting ready to leave for the Halloween dance at the college. They were going early because Pop was on the committee to decorate the gym where the dance was going to be held.

Mom was wearing a black leotard with a high neck and long sleeves. She was just fastening a floor-length skirt of bright orange-and-red wool, which she had woven herself, around her waist. And she had lots of jangling gold jewelry around her neck. She looked really great and not too spooky at all in spite of the fact that it was Halloween.

"Sara love, are you really going to stay home tonight? No trick-or-treating? No party?"

"That's right," I said. I was sitting, all crumpled up, on a straw mat on the floor of my room. That was how I felt inside, too. Crumpled up. Like a sheet of fresh white tissue paper that somebody had taken in their fist and squashed into something the size of a ping-pong ball.

Mom crouched down beside me. "It's a pity.

You had such a good idea for a costume. And you worked so hard on that Statue of Liberty crown."

I shook my head. "Doesn't matter."

"Couldn't you still arrange to go out trick-or-treating with some of the other kids, maybe some of the kids who are going to be at the party? Or Toby could go trick-or-treating with you and then take you over to Roddy's party and we'd pick you up when it's over. Toby won't mind getting to his party a little later. He feels sort of responsible for this mess between you and Glenda."

"No," I interrupted irritably. "I can't do that. Don't you see, that's exactly what Glenda's going to do. She'll probably go trick-or-treating with those kids and then *she'll* go to Roddy's party. Oooh, I have a good mind to phone her right this minute and tell her they never wanted her there in the first place and only invited her at the last minute because they knew I wouldn't come without her!" And I began scrambling to my feet, thinking that was exactly what I'd do.

But Inez put a firm hand on my shoulder. "No Sara. Don't do that. Telling Glenda the truth about Roddy's invitation would be very cruel and hurtful."

"But look how she's hurt me! 'You stick to *your* family; I'll stick to *my* family.' And all the time I thought we understood and even liked each other's families. I really *did* like her family. Going over to er house to make alphabet-burgers in her mother's kitchen was like stepping back into Aunt Minna's kitchen in Crestview. I even told Glenda how I felt because I thought she was my friend. And she used to tell me how interesting she thought you and Pop were and how she admired the clever way we did things at our house."

Inez just kept watching me with a worried frown.

"And now," I went on, "I see that she only pretended to understand what it was like for me, because she needed to have a friend. Because nobody else in the whole neighborhood would have anything to do with her. Now she'll have plenty of friends and she won't need me. And she'll never even know that the only reason she got them was because of me."

Mom put her arm around my shoulders. "No Sara, it won't work that way. If there is some reason they didn't want her before, they won't be so quick to accept her now."

"Yes, they will," I insisted. "She'll tell them all how kooky we are. How you painted the guest room ceiling black and how none of us sleep in regular beds and how you and Drew eat raw meat with raw eggs on top. And they'll all make terrible fun of me. Oh, can't we move back to California?" I pleaded. "It's going to be awful here without any friends at all."

"Sara," Inez soothed, "please don't decide this

minute how everything is going to be from now c
You're very upset—and you're mixed up, too."

"All I know is I hate Glenda," I exploded. "I just
hate her!"

"Don't say that, Sara. Glenda really was your
friend in many ways. But perhaps it took too much
courage for her to be your friend all the way. Just
remember that you were the one who told *us* to be
patient because people around here weren't ready
for changes. Maybe Glenda wasn't as ready as you
thought she was. Maybe it was too hard for her to
'understand'; maybe she always had too many problems of her own."

I just sat there thinking bitterly that it was easy
for Mom to be so understanding toward Glenda;
she hadn't just lost her only friend.

It wasn't the same for Inez and Drew as it was
for me. They had made lots of friends among the
people who taught out at the college. Toby had it
easy, too, because he liked a lot of the kids who
worked on the school newspaper and who came to
Havenhurst High from all over the surrounding
area, not just from our part of Havenhurst.

Just then Drew stuck his head in the doorway of
my room. "Ready to go, I? How's Sara?"

"I'm okay," I said glumly.

"Not very," Mom said, giving Pop a quick look.
She turned to me. "Look, Sara. Toby will stay with
you until nine o'clock. I'll phone from the college

...at ten to, to see how you are. If you're still
...set I'll come back before Toby leaves. I wouldn't
...ven go now except I've promised to do the special-
effects part of the decorating. Is that plan okay?"

I nodded. Mom touched her lips to the top of
my head and went off downstairs to tell Toby the
plan. Right after that she and Pop left.

It was still early, only about seven thirty. All afternoon the little kids had kept coming around,
ringing the doorbell to get candy for trick-or-treat.
They traipsed up the steps in their funny little costumes, lugging great big orange-and-black shopping
bags for people to dump the candy in. Some of
them were so small they couldn't even reach the
doorbell. Most of them came with their mothers
who waited for them out on the sidewalk. But now
they had dwindled down to a trickle. Toby had
been staying downstairs for the past half hour so
he could answer the door.

I went downstairs slowly. Toby was sitting in the
living room with a book in his lap. He looked up as
I came into the room.

"Hi, Sara," he said. "Are you sore at me?"

"Why should I be?"

"Well, I'm afraid my bringing Bruce over here
this afternoon had a lot to do with busting up your
Halloween plans."

"No, Toby. It isn't your fault—it's Glenda's. Or
maybe it's just the way things are. Anyhow, Toby,

what I came downstairs to tell you is that I'm okay So why don't you go on over to your party now?"

Toby shook his head. "I told Inez I'd be here till nine o'clock."

"Look Toby, that's stupid. I'm as okay now as I'm going to be at nine. When Mom phones, I'll tell her I made you go even though you didn't want to. Except I know you really do. I mean it, Toby. Please don't hang around on my account."

"Nope. Nothing doing."

But I could tell Toby wasn't going to hold out for long. I went back up to my room and about ten minutes later he came up and said if I was *really* okay maybe he *would* leave.

"Boy," I said, "you're harder to get rid of than the itch from a whole can of itching powder."

"Okay," Toby cautioned, "but one thing I want you to promise."

"What's that?"

"No opening the door to any trick-or-treaters who come around from now on."

"What should I do? Suppose they get sore and pull a trick?"

"I already took care of that. I put all the Halloween candy in a big brown bag and attached it to the outside doorknob with a sign that says, 'Please take some and leave the rest for others.' That ought to do it."

I nodded.

"Take care now, Sara, and be good."

"You, too," I called after him as Toby bounded down the stairs and out the front door.

I sat in my room for about fifteen minutes mulling the whole awful mess with Glenda over and over in my mind. Every now and then my eye fell on my Statue of Liberty crown. It was really beautiful, each spike perfect, and exactly the same number of spikes as on the real Statue of Liberty crown. I got up off the floor and put it on and looked at myself in the mirror.

"Well, why not?" I thought. "It's Halloween and I've got my costume and my mask ready. Why shouldn't I have a little fun just going around and trick-or-treating by myself." I didn't need Fat Glenda. I didn't need her or anyone else.

So I began to get dressed in my costume, putting on a pair of warm slacks and three sweaters under my bedsheet-robe because it was really getting chilly out now. I could hear the wind rattling the bare branches of the big tree outside my window and making them scrape and scratch against the glass like wild things trying to get in.

At last I was ready. I took my flashlight, which was supposed to be my Statue of Liberty torch, and a small paper shopping bag for candy and stuff, and a UNICEF canister to try to collect some money in. I took my house key, too, so I could get back in before the others returned.

I went out and closed the front door, and first thing I did was to trip on the front steps b cause of the long, loose bedsheet and the mask ove. my eyes, which made it hard to see where I was going. That made me lose my balance, and my crown got knocked crooked. I felt so stupid. But after I straightened out my crown and hitched up my bedsheet a little higher under my sash, I was okay.

I started down the street. It was now dark outside and there weren't many people around. The little kids had all been taken home for supper a long time ago and maybe the big kids hadn't started out yet.

After the first doorbell I rang, where they put a whole quarter in my UNICEF canister, I began to feel much better. People were really nice. They all seemed to have lots of candy around and after they gave me a nickel or a dime for UNICEF, they said I should take some candy, too, as my "reward" for the "good work" I was doing.

One lady was giving out big, shiny red apples instead of candy to the kids who rang her doorbell. She said apples were much more healthful and wouldn't cause cavities. She was right of course. But she must have had to buy just bushels of apples for Halloween.

At one house a man answered the door. He seemed sleepy and grumpy at first. He said he n't have any small change for UNICEF, but he ered me a dollar bill.

"You don't have to give that much," I said.

"Haven't got any change," he muttered, fishing around in his pockets and coming up with nothing but a small bunch of keys. "Tell you what. You take this and give me fifty cents change."

"I can't," I said. "It's a sealed collection carton and I haven't got any other money on me."

"Well, that's the best I can do, girlie. But if you want to come back later, half of this dollar is yours."

"All right," I said. "I will."

"Oh, and have a candy." He held out a box of chocolates, each in its own little fluted paper cup. The box was pretty well picked over and I didn't really want one of the stale-looking chocolates. But he had such a sad, tired look on his face that I rummaged around in the empty papers and found one and took it. The house was all dead and quiet behind him, like no wife or children lived there with him, although maybe once, a long time ago, they had.

I had been trick-or-treating for about three-quarters of an hour and had made a circle around the neighborhood. I wasn't far from home, so I decided to stop at our house, leave the apple and all the candy I'd collected, and get the change for the man with the dollar bill.

I had just come around the corner onto ...gerfield Road when I saw this whole bunch of ... coming toward me. They all seemed to be in c... tume except for the one in front. It was a larg... figure in dark pants and a dark jacket, and it looked as if it were running straight for me.

I got a little frightened remembering what Glenda had said about things getting rough in Havenhurst after dark on Halloween and about needing somebody to protect us when we went trick-or-treating.

Then the others seemed to stop or drop back but the figure kept coming closer and I still couldn't make out whether it was a man or a boy or what. The jacket it wore had a hood that fitted closely over the head and was pulled together around the face with a string or an elastic.

Then the person running toward me opened its mouth and shrieked, "Sara!" And I knew right away that it was Glenda.

We met under the street lamp and I could see the round moon of her face, her forehead popping with little beads of sweat even in the Halloween cold. Her eyes were wide open and terrified-looking.

"Sara," she panted, "Sara, you better come quick."

"Why?" I said, gaping. "What's happened?"

"They threw eggs at your house and then they

inside the yard and started tearing down those
pipes."

She grabbed both my arms.

"Oh please, Sara, come quickly. I'm *so* glad I
found you!"

12

BY THE time I got back to our house, with Glenda puffing along behind me and dropping farther and farther behind, there were about a million kids gathered there, including the ones who had come part of the way with Glenda to get me. Oh well, maybe not a million. But twelve or fourteen anyway.

It was impossible to know who was who because everybody had costumes and masks on. Except Glenda, of course.

Somebody in a wolf-man's face-mask, with fangs and make-believe blood dripping down its chin, was just coming out of our yard, saying, "Well, they *nearly* wrecked it, all right. I'd say about half of it's still standing. It's hard to know with a crazy-looking thing like that."

I had taken my mask off so I could see where I was running and as soon as the wolf-man saw me he came over and took his mask off.

It was Roddy Fenton, of course. I'd known that, even with his mask on, just from hearing his voice. I had such mixed-up feelings about Roddy I didn't

ow whether I was glad to see him or furious at
im.

He grinned. "I see Glenda found you. Say, whatever happened between you two? I thought you
were going trick-or-treating together."

"We had a fight," I said, glancing back over my
shoulder to indicate Glenda, and not even caring
who knew it. "I went trick-or-treating by myself.
What's been going on around here anyway? Who
made this awful mess?"

I hadn't even gotten around to the front of the
house yet, but there were broken eggs all over the
sidewalk and from what I could see of "Stovepipes"
it didn't look anything like it had that afternoon
when Toby had been up on top trying to finish it
for Pop.

Before Roddy could answer, Mary Lou came
rushing over to me. She was dressed in a Mother
Goose costume with a tall, pointy black hat. "Oh
Sara," she gasped, "you should see what they did to
your house. The whole front's just *pelted* with eggs.
Every window's all covered with goo and slime and
bits and pieces of broken shell, and there's yellow
running down the clapboard. It's just disgusting!
Makes my flesh creep. It really does." Mary Lou
backed off a little. "Oh, I like your costume. Is it
homemade? It looks homemade but it's real clever."

I reached up and fingered my crown. Some of
the spikes were broken and flopping over. "I'm
afraid it's falling apart," I said in a flat voice.

Glenda had caught up with me and now stood panting at my side. She touched my arm shyly. "Don't feel bad, Sara. They threw eggs at the windows of our house, too, and at some of the other houses on the street. Although I don't think any house got it as bad as yours did."

Looking around the yard, I believed her.

"That's because nobody was home," she went on. "My father was in the living room when an egg hit our picture window. He ran right out and— guess what? They were throwing the eggs from a car and he got hit right smack in the face with one."

The other kids all snickered. It was funny really. I could just see Mr. Waite, with his horn-rimmed eyeglasses and his small black moustache all runny with egg.

"But who did it?" I asked, looking around at the circle of faces. Most of them had their masks off now. I recognized Cathanne and Patty and a couple of other boys and girls from school. They were probably all part of the crowd that was going to Roddy's party. "Doesn't anybody know?"

Everybody shrugged.

I could hear Glenda breathing hard next to me. All of a sudden she burst out at Roddy. "Oh, come on, Roddy," she said, glaring straight at him. "You do so know who did it. So why don't you tell Sara?"

Roddy turned an angry red and made a ferocious face at Glenda. "What are you talking about? I

141

don't know one single thing about it. Why should I?" He was so angry his voice broke into shrill splintery sounds. "But I'll tell you one thing, kiddo," he said, jabbing a finger at Glenda's face. "Even if I did know, I'm no squealer. Not like you!"

Then he turned to me. "Cross my heart, Sara, it was some kids in a car, so you know it wasn't us. We were all out trick-or-treating and we came by your house thinking maybe you'd come along. There must have been about four or five of them in the car. After they finished throwing the eggs, they piled out and ran into the yard and started climbing that tower or whatever it is and then they started pulling it down."

"It's true, Sara," Mary Lou echoed from behind Roddy. "We all got here just in time to scare them off. We could tell there was nobody home at your house or somebody surely would have been outside screaming at them, so that's when I said, 'Why don't we go over to Glenda's and see if Sara's there.' So some of us did and when we got to Glenda's house she was there all right but you weren't, and she said she'd go out and look for you."

I glanced at Glenda sharply. "How'd you know where I was?"

"Oh," she looked away for a moment. "I saw you go by in your costume a few minutes after eight. You were walking on the other side of the street. I just happened to be looking out the window. You rang some doorbells on our block and then you turned the corner. I figured you had to be somewhere right around the neighborhood."

"It sounds," I said coldly, "as if you were spying on me."

"Sara, I was not spying!"

"Oh, she probably was," Roddy interrupted in a singsong voice. "She's a great one for spying." He turned to Glenda. "Why don't you tell Sara what a famous little detective you are?"

"Why don't *you* tell her about your brother and his friends?" Glenda mimicked in return. "They were probably the ones who threw the eggs and busted up 'Stovepipes.' "

I looked from Glenda to Roddy and back again, but I couldn't make much sense out of what they were saying. All the other kids were just standing there, watching and listening the way I was.

Roddy took a threatening step toward Glenda. "That was *not* my brother who was over here. It wasn't his car. I ought to know my own brother's car. Anyhow he went to a party all the way across town with some of the kids from Havenhurst High. He left the house a couple of hours ago."

"It still could have been him, in somebody else's car," Glenda said stubbornly. "He was here in this very yard only this afternoon, looking over the place. I saw him myself." She was really brave to keep insisting because Roddy looked as if he was getting ready to hit her. "And if it wasn't him, I bet

143

it was those no-good friends of his—Beast and that crowd. Everybody knows they're nothing but a bunch of punks."

Roddy stepped up very close to Glenda and his words exploded in her face. "Bruce does not go around with Beast anymore!" Roddy's hands flew to Glenda's throat and began to encircle the collar of her zipper-jacket. "And you lay off my brother, you squealing rat! Hear me? For once and for all, lay off!"

"He's going to choke her," Mary Lou shrilled. "Somebody stop him. *Please*."

I was already shoving my way between them. "Cut it out," I said irritably. "What's all this about, anyway? Can't somebody tell me? I know who Bruce is. But who's Beast?"

Cathanne, the girl with the long red hair and the sharp nose, tapped me on the shoulder.

"Beast is a big fat guy with pimples. He dropped out of school last June. But it coulda been him and some of his crew did this job tonight. I don't know." She turned to Patty who was standing at her side. "What do you think?"

Patty nodded. "It coulda. It definitely coulda."

Roddy had let go of Glenda now and was leaning back against the fence that encircled our yard. Glenda still stood in the same spot where Roddy had started to choke her. I could see she was trembling.

"Okay," I said, "maybe it *was* this kid Beast who

did it. But what's all this stuff about Glenda and Roddy's brother? What's she got to do with Bruce anyway?"

"Go on, tell her," Roddy said to Glenda with a smirk on his face. "Tell her what a squealer you are."

Glenda stood there a minute with her face all red and sweaty. Then she ripped back the hood of her jacket. "All right, I will! 'Cause I'm not ashamed of it. I did see him steal that car. And I'm not sorry I told."

There was a little chorus of gasps from the kids standing around.

"He didn't steal it," Roddy snarled.

"Oh no? Then why did the police find him and Beast in it later that night all the way out at Fish Harbor? Hmmm?"

"He only borrowed it!"

"Did Bruce really take somebody's car?" I asked Glenda.

"He did, Sara. Honest he did. I saw it myself. It happened last November, about a year ago. I was coming home from school real late one afternoon. It was nearly dark out. I saw Bruce get in this car in Mr. Ellacott's driveway and fiddle around a little and then he got it started and he drove away. I thought maybe he was just borrowing it, too, at first. But when I got home and mentioned it to my mother, she telephoned Mr. Ellacott and he didn't even know it was gone till he ran outside to look."

"Then what happened?"

"Then my mother said we had to go to the police station and report it. And we did."

"Her mother, her mother," Roddy murmured sourly. "Her mother's really a pip." Suddenly he leaned forward and grabbed my shoulder, practically knocking me off my feet. "Hey, I'll bet she never even told you that her mother got up that petition against your family on account of all this junk in the yard and whatever. . . ."

Roddy waved an arm at the wreckage of "Stovepipes" just over the fence. "I'll bet you didn't even know that, did you? What've you got to say about your fat girlfriend now?"

Glenda's eyes were fixed on me. They looked dark and frightened.

"I don't think her being fat has anything to do with any of the things you just said about her," I said stiffly to Roddy.

Roddy waved his arm as if to say, "Okay, okay."

"And about the petition," I went on, "I already found out about that, so you're not telling me anything new. You can't make Glenda responsible for everything her mother does."

I could read the gratitude in Glenda's eyes for that. Roddy just looked disappointed.

Of course, I still had to have it out with Glenda about whether she knew about the petition all along, but I didn't want to do that in front of everybody. Even though I was still partly angry at

Glenda, I had to admit she was having a pretty hard time of it with Roddy and all.

"Say, Roddy," Mary Lou piped up, "it's getting late. Why don't we get on over to your house for the party?"

Roddy looked surly. "No. I'm not leaving here until she takes back what she said about Bruce being the one who threw those eggs tonight." And he looked menacingly at Glenda again.

"I didn't say it *was* him," Glenda protested. "I said it could have been."

"Look," Roddy said, "it wasn't Bruce and that's that. And the only reason he took Mr. Ellacott's car that time was because somebody dared him to."

"What he did was still against the law," Glenda said. "And he didn't end up going to jail for it or anything. He only got a warning."

"That was bad enough. The police were checking up on him plenty for a long time."

"Well, he deserved it."

"Listen," Roddy said, "you just take back what you said about Bruce throwing the eggs."

"I only said 'maybe.' "

"Take it back."

"I didn't say he . . ."

"Yes you did."

Glenda dropped her head so nobody could see her face. "Well . . . about that . . . maybe I was wrong. Maybe he . . ."

Glenda stopped abruptly. The headlights of a

car, driving slowly and very close to the curb, swept down the street toward where we stood. Somebody screamed, "They're coming back! Look out, everybody." And we all began to run, thinking about flying eggs, and Beast, and the other big kids who might be with him.

And then the car stopped in front of the house and the headlights dimmed, and I saw that it was Inez and Drew in the borrowed station wagon.

They got out of the car and at first they didn't seem to notice the egg all over the house, the wreckage of "Stovepipes," or Glenda, or even the bunch of kids standing around on the sidewalk. They just seemed to see me, and Inez ran over to me and said, "Sara baby, thank heaven you're safe. I rang and rang the phone and there was no answer. No Toby. No you. What on earth's been happening here?"

13

IT SEEMED as though Mom and Pop and Glenda and I, and Toby who got a lift home in the car with Bruce (who, Toby said, really had been at the party with him all evening) were up most of the night scrubbing the egg off the house.

Toby and Pop kept looking anxiously over toward "Stovepipes" while they brought ladders and started scrubbing the upper part of the house. They had both been tight-lipped when they first saw the damage. But once they got past the shock they began to talk quietly about "Stovepipes," and I could tell they were already thinking about the next day and about reconstructing it.

Glenda insisted on helping clean the egg off the house because she said she had a lot of experience and also because, if you didn't do it right away, it dried on and was even harder to get off.

When I asked Glenda if her mother had phoned the police after their house was hit by eggs, Glenda said she certainly had. But as far as she knew, the police had never arrived because they always got so many calls on Halloween and it was almost impossible to ever catch the culprits. "But don't worry.

My mother'll go down to the station house tomorrow and make a full report. She always does."

While we were rinsing out the rags down in the basement Glenda confessed to me that she had known about her mother starting the petition.

"But how could I have told you that, Sara? You'd probably have gotten so mad you'd have left me flat. Right? And even if *you* didn't get too mad, when your folks found out they'd have made you stop going around with me. Then what would I have done?"

I was really beginning to see how trapped Glenda had been.

"So now I know why you've been having all that trouble with Roddy, too," I said.

"That's right."

"But why did you have to get so mad and hang up on me when I phoned you? That didn't make things any better."

"Because, Sara, after seeing Bruce Fenton over at your place, I was scared. I was afraid he'd told you and Toby about the way I ratted on him and got him into trouble with the police. When you called me on the phone, I figured you were going to ask me about that next. I guess I really was ashamed of it, and of the way all the kids called me a 'squealer.' I didn't want you to know about that *or* the petition. So I just didn't say anything." She sighed. "I guess that was pretty dumb of me."

I nodded. "It sure was."

All this time Glenda was leaning over the sink and rinsing out rags and wringing them dry as if her life depended upon it. "You know," she said, without looking up at me, "even though it sounds awful to say it, in a way I'm glad they threw all those eggs at your house tonight. Because when Mary Lou came to tell me, it gave me a chance to go out and look for you . . . and for us to be friends again." She looked up. "If we are, that is."

I wasn't really ready to commit myself about that. So instead I said, "Oh look, Glenda, you won't have too much trouble about friends from now on. You even apologized to Roddy, sort of."

Glenda shook her head. "Uh-uh. That won't make any difference. The kids around here never liked me, even before I got Bruce into trouble. They always teased me about being so fat and clumsy. Roddy was usually the ringleader. But even without him to tell them, the kids were just awful to me. The girls were always sort of mean and stuck-up. And the boys didn't want to go around with me because other boys teased them about it."

"Is that why you told on Bruce, Glenda?"

She looked at me startled. "What do you mean?"

"Well, you know, to get even."

"Honestly, I never thought of it that way."

"But it could be true, couldn't it?"

Glenda nodded very slowly. "In a way. I suppose so." She plopped down on an old crate as if she was suddenly very tired. But she seemed to be thinking hard about something. "Oh boy," she said after awhile, "if that's the way it is, I'm going to be in trouble for the rest of my life. Because I won't have you around for very long, Sara. Didn't you say once that your father's teaching job out at the college was only for a year? That means you'll be going back to California next June, won't you?"

I *had* heard Mom and Pop discussing whether Drew's contract might be renewed for another year but, of course, it was much too early to tell.

"Well that's how it looks," I said, remembering how only last night I'd been so angry at Glenda I was praying to go back to California right then and there.

Glenda just nodded miserably. "See, that's what I mean. I'm still going to have all the same problems. And every time I get unhappy and upset like this, I eat even more and gain another five or ten pounds."

It really was awful for Glenda. Whoever got the idea that fat people were always jolly and happy? And that's when I got *my* idea.

"Glenda," I pounced, "I've got it!"

"Got what?"

"An idea. So you won't have to worry about getting new friends even if I do have to leave here in June."

"What's that?"

"Well, between now and June you won't be unhappy and upset, so you won't have to eat a lot to make yourself feel better when you're worried or when your feelings are hurt. Because Toby and Inez and Drew and I will be your friends and we'll help you. And maybe we can ask Inez about her raw-food diet. You have to admit that Inez and Drew are about the thinnest people you ever met."

Glenda nodded. But she still didn't seem to be convinced.

"In fact, you could start eating all your meals over at my house so you wouldn't be tempted by your mother's stews and things. And we'd all watch you and try to think up interesting new things to eat that wouldn't be fattening. And see that there was no nibbling in between meals and all that. And maybe by June you'll be thin."

"Oh Sara, do you think I could?"

"You could, Glenda, you could." I raised my right arm to show it was the truth. "And the first thing that has to go is alphabet-burgers. Did you know that a 3-ounce hamburger has 245 calories in it? And that's without the roll, which has about 150. And without the alphabet part, which we don't even *know* how many calories it could have . . ."

And that's how come Toby and Glenda and I ate Z-burgers for lunch the day after Halloween—in *our* kitchen this time! It was to be the last of the alphabet-burgers. And Z stood for—guess what— zero-burgers!

Zero meant there was not only nothing on top of

the hamburgers; there was nothing in the middle either. I have to admit it was Toby's idea.

We shaped the hamburgers like doughnuts, with holes in the center, and then grilled them. That must have cut the calories down to about 200 anyway.

Frankly, we would have had to limp our way through the last five or six letters of the alphabet. Just think how hard it would have been to get ideas for X-burgers and Y-burgers. So we cheated and went directly to Z. Anyhow, I figured the sooner we called it quits with alphabet-burgers, the sooner we could get Glenda on her new diet.

Maybe you can think of something better for Z-burgers. If you do—or if you get any really great ideas for Glenda's diet—why don't you let me know?

I expect to be here in Havenhurst for a while.